SHEEP

ALSO BY VALERIE HOBBS

Defiance

Letting Go of Bobby James, or
How I Found My Self of Steam

Stefan's Story

Sonny's War

Tender

Charlie's Run

Carolina Crow Girl

How Far Would You Have Gotten If I Hadn't
Called You Back?

Get It While It's Hot. Or Not.

VALERIE HOBBS

SHEEP

SQUARE
FISH

Farrar Straus Giroux
New York

*Heartfelt thanks to Maggie Desruisseaux, Alex Bush, and
Jacob Coffey for their encouragement and good advice as I
struggled to become a dog.*

**SQUARE
FISH**

An Imprint of Macmillan

Library of Congress Cataloging-in-Publication Data
Hobbs, Valerie.
    Sheep / Valerie Hobbs.
        p. cm.
    Summary: After a fire destroys the farm where he was born, a young border
collie acquires a series of owners and learns about life as he seeks a home and
longs to fulfill his life's purpose of shepherding sheep.
    ISBN-13: 978-0-312-56116-1
    ISBN-10: 0-312-56116-4
    1. Border collie—Juvenile fiction. [1. Border collie—Fiction. 2. Adventure
and adventurers—Fiction. 3. Dogs—Fiction. 4. Sheep—Fiction.] I. Title.

PZ10.3.H6463She 2006
[Fic]—dc22

                                                    2005046356

First published in the United States by Farrar, Straus and Giroux
Square Fish logo designed by Filomena Tuosto
Designed by Robbin Gourley
First Square Fish Edition: May 2009
10 9 8 7 6 5 4 3 2 1
www.squarefishbooks.com

To my grandson, Diego Joaquin Salgado

SHEEP

1

MY NAME IS JACK, but it wasn't always. I've had so many names I can't even remember them all. Some names were good, some were bad. Some I don't like to remember. But I like the name Jack just fine. It's the one Luke gave me, and he's my best friend.

Until I found Luke, life was a long, hard road. I'd traveled too many days on an empty stomach, slept too many nights in the rain, gone too long without a friend. I was giving up hope, which is about the worst thing you can do. Hope is everything.

When I was a youngster, I was filled with hope. But I was trouble, too. Trouble with a capital T, Mom said. Always poking my nose where it didn't belong, getting into mischief. Nobody thought I'd amount to much. But young as I was, I knew better. There was a job for me out there in the world, something big and important. All I had to do was find out what it was. Meanwhile, I had to stay out of trouble.

Hanging around the ranch all day with Mom was downright boring. There was only so much you could think up to do without getting into trouble. And if you were *real* bad, well then Mom made you take a nap. She sure didn't think I was ready for anything big and important. So I was counting on Bob.

Bob smelled like smoke and hay, that's what I remember. Cooked eggs, coffee, toast crumbs, applesauce, pig meat, soap. I loved him so much it hurt not to show it. As soon as I heard him coming, I'd want to race out and throw myself against his legs, bark and yip, run in circles like a fool. But I wouldn't let myself, not then. I had to show him that I could be counted on. That I was ready for the sheep. So while the others whined and jumped and tried to get his attention, I'd stand real still, cock my head just so, and give him my best sheep eye. That's the look you give the sheep to make them behave.

And then I'd just lose it, I'd get so excited I'd be all over him. Yapping, licking his big, rough hands. I just couldn't help myself.

Bob had dark things on his mind in those days, you could tell by the way his forehead bunched all up. There were lots of things to worry about on a California sheep ranch. He wasn't humming or talking real low to my dad and the fellas the way he did sometimes. He'd pat a nose stuck under his hand, but it was like he wasn't there. He'd forget things, too. Then Ellen would come running out of the house. "Bob? You forgot your gloves! Bob? You forgot your hat!" Ellen and Bob loved each other a whole lot, even a pup could tell. But things weren't right on the ranch. None of the fellas knew why, except maybe Old Dex, the lead dog, and he wasn't saying. There was talk of selling, but we pups didn't understand about that.

As far as I knew, every day was the same and that was how it would always be. Bob would come for the fellas, slapping his gloves together, blowing clouds through the cold, dark air. He'd fill their bowls with food and water and set them down where he knew the fellas wanted them. Then, while we pups swarmed around his ankles, he'd fill one big bowl for us. The second he set it down, we'd attack like a pack of ill-mannered bloodhounds. Even I would forget about making a good impression. I'd push and shove and keep my nose right in there. A day without a full belly wasn't a day I wanted to live.

Well, that's how you think when you're young, before you see the long road ahead. Full-belly days are all you know.

When breakfast was over, Bob would round up the fellas for the workday. Old Dex would lead the way to the truck, followed by Dad. They'd jump in first, then the others behind them. Bob would latch the tailgate and climb into the cab. I'd watch the rusty red truck drive away, hoping that, just once, it would stop. That Bob would remember he'd forgotten one last thing: me. But the truck always kept going to that place at the edge of the land where it disappeared.

The rest of the day I'd try to keep myself busy, chasing gophers, playing sticks with my brothers, taking long naps with Mom. But even in my sleep I'd listen for the truck, waiting for the fellas to return and talk about their day.

Oh, they never said much. Work was work, you know. When you're as good as they were, you don't need to brag. You simply go out and do what you were born to do. That's the way it is with Border collies, the way it's been for centuries. I thought I'd never be one of them, except in name. Never get to run with the sheep. I'd always be a mama's boy, a pesky pup, a reject.

And then it came, a day that started like all the others and changed my life forever. Bob said, "Come, boy." And he meant me.

Me? My ears went straight up, but the rest of me froze. Me?

"Come, boy," Bob said again, in that low voice, so kind. And then I was off like a shot, straight up into the back of the truck, my tail trying its best to wag my hind end clean off.

Old Dex just rolled his eyes at me, the way dogs do. Well, you wouldn't know.

We rode out through heaven, grass so green and lush you felt like chewing on it. I raced from one side of the truck bed to the other, sticking my nose between the slats, while the land rolled on and on, not a house or barn anywhere. The air was clean and cold and filled with what I had no name for. Excitement is probably what you'd call it. But it was more than that, though I didn't know it then. I figured if all we did was ride out to where the world ended and back again, well, that would be enough for me.

That was before I saw the sheep. Sheep everywhere! The truck stopped, and they closed in all around us like a big gray woolly blanket, bawling and baaing, stinking like, well, like sheep. Bob hopped down out of the cab and pushed his way through them to the back of the truck. When he lowered the tailgate, the fellas jumped down, working the sheep the minute they hit the ground, rounding them up without even trying.

I hung back, a little soft in the belly, if you know what I mean. Nervous. They were bigger than I was, every last one, and so many I couldn't count them, more sheep than I thought there were in the whole wide world.

Well, you didn't have to count them, though I didn't know it then. You just sort of *felt* them, Dad said. That was how you knew when one went missing. You felt it somewhere inside you. Sounded crazy to me. The smell was bad enough. But *feeling* sheep? I didn't like the sound of that. I figured if worst came to worst, and the sheep wouldn't do what I wanted, well, I'd just bite them. But I learned soon enough that wasn't the way. Only as a last resort would a dog bite a sheep.

You should have seen Dad and Old Dex, how they got those woolly guys all moving in the same direction. You could tell the sheep didn't like it. They'd have to run a little, which they hated, so they grumbled the whole time. One old ewe really had her back up. She turned, frowned at the dogs, and tried to hold her ground. It came down to her and Old Dex then, him with his snout low, ready to leap left or right. And that eye he gave her! It made you shiver just to watch.

The old lady just couldn't hold out against that eye. She gave Old Dex one last haughty look, then turned away and trotted off after the others, her fat little tail between her legs.

I ran back and forth, trying to look like I knew what I was doing, practicing my sheep eye. The sheep ignored me, like I was a pesky fly. After a while Dad told me to calm down, but I couldn't. I'd gotten a taste of what life was all about, and I didn't want to miss a second of it.

"Keep your eye on Old Dex," Dad said. "You've got a chance to learn from a master." And so I did. Wherever Old Dex went, that was where I'd try to be. But it wasn't easy. One second he'd be racing full out alongside the flock, then he'd stop, ears up, and cut the other way. Bob would call an order from a long way off, telling you what he wanted, and you had to do it right then. It was tricky, but when you got the sheep going the way they were supposed to, like a big muddy gray river rolling across the land, you were happy inside. It was better than a good meal, better than a rubdown, even better than Mom saying you were her own best boy (well, she said it to my brothers, too, I know she did). When the sheep were right, you had that deep down good feeling that you were making a difference. You were doing what you were meant to do, what you believed in, what you were really good at.

I'll tell you, nothing in the world is better than that.

The day came to an end too soon for me. We all bounded back up into the truck, and as the land took that last lick of the sun, we headed home. I'd learned more than my head could hold. I knew for certain my purpose in this life, and I was ready to do it, flat out, with all my heart.

But it was not to be. One day, when we'd gathered all the sheep and were driving them down to the barns, a storm rose up out of nowhere. The wind began to moan and cry. Lightning struck all around, and the dry grass caught fire. I saw Bob, riding his horse, Appie, look behind us to where the sky was turning orange. I heard him call an order. Then he pulled his bandanna up over his nose, gave Appie a slap, and raced ahead. We dogs went into top speed, pushing those sheep, even nipping their heels when they wouldn't run. Something was crackling behind us. I turned and saw the tongues of flame licking, racing to catch up with us.

"Don't look back!" Old Dex barked. "Run!"

I ran. Ran until I thought I couldn't run another step, until I couldn't see the sheep for the smoke, and then I ran some more.

2

THE RANCH WAS LOST, most of it anyway. Bob sold off the wool, then a lot of the sheep. It was a sad time for us all, but we worked when Bob wanted us to, we did our part.

Then one morning months later, instead of the old red truck, there came a different truck. This one was big and black and had wire all around the back of it; we soon learned why. While Ellen cried in Bob's arms, we pups were rounded up and put into the big cage. You never heard such howling and barking, dogs everywhere and men chasing after them. I was so curious, they snatched me up first. Mom went wild. She ran in circles, up to Bob, then back to the truck, barking and crying. Where was Dad? Dad would save us, wouldn't he? Then, as the truck pulled away, I saw him. He was standing off to the side, next to Old Dex. I yelled, "Dad!" So did my brothers and sister, all yelping and barking at once. Dad lifted his snout. I think by that he meant for us to be brave, but my heart was breaking and I couldn't be brave. I whined and yipped and cried until I had no voice left.

Where were they taking us? And why did they leave our moms and dads behind? Why didn't they want Old Dex, the best of us all? How would we learn to herd the sheep without him? And where were Bob and Ellen? Why did they let the black truck take us away?

The rest I'd rather forget. Somewhere on that dark journey, I lost a brother, my sister, all my friends, and then my last brother, the runt. And I was alone, caged like the lowest form of criminal, going . . . where? I couldn't begin to guess.

Exhausted, I slept as much as I could, hearing only the clink and clank of metal as I went from one cage to another. At last, I opened my eyes and found myself in a space hardly big enough to turn around in, staring through glass. Across the way a bunch of mice were running like crazy around a little wheel. Next to me a pair of beagle pups were curled up together asleep. Where was I?

I yipped and turned in circles, scratched at the glass. Nobody came. The mice never turned their pink noses, never stopped running. I had to settle myself down, figure out where I was. I could see it was a place with lots of animals. Alongside the mice was another glass box, this one filled with water and the strangest creatures moving through it. Gold and blue and green, with round, staring eyes and wavy tails.

Well, I'd never seen fish before. You can imagine what I thought. The fish and mice were so busy, I could forget for a little while that I was behind glass, too. But every now and then a big green-and-yellow bird hanging from the ceiling would screech, "Abandon ship!" and scare me half to death.

After a while a man came and opened my door. "Here we go, pup," he said, and lifted me out. I was so grateful to be free of that box, I slobbered all over his hand. He scratched my neck. Then he slung me over his shoulder and carried me through the whole place. It was something all right, filled with animals I'd never seen the likes of in my life. Not only fish but snakes and lizards, too. Well, I'd run into a few of those on the ranch, but not such big guys. One lizard gave me the eye, turning his big green head real slow as we passed. Gave me the creeps. But all the while a bunch of canaries were singing their hearts out. It made you feel as if everything would turn out all right after all.

That's when I saw the water. A whole tub of it, and it was meant for me.

"In you go," the man said. My feet started scrambling through air. I cried like the baby I was, but it didn't do one bit of good.

"It's all right," the man said, and plop in the water I

went. "You'll feel lots better when you've had a nice warm bath."

I'll bet you've heard that one before.

Well, I knew that if I'd needed a bath, Bob would have given me one. And now I knew why he didn't. Baths are terrible things. Soapsuds in your eyes and up your nose, making you sneeze. Bubbles popping and snapping in your ears, your feet slipping out beneath you.

Afterward, I couldn't stop shaking. Couldn't get all that water off. I really thought I'd lost the good smell of me forever.

Dinner wasn't much better. Hard little pellets. Tasted like the paper bag they came out of. And then back in that darned glass box. I folded my paws over my head and went to sleep longing for home. I didn't like this new place. I don't think the other pups did either. The beagles slept all the time. I think they were depressed.

It was downright humiliating for a dog to be stuck like a fish or a snake inside a glass box, especially a dog of my proud lineage. I kept thinking about Dad, about the way he lifted his snout. I was trying to be brave, but I couldn't help wondering what would become of me. Why did the man keep me in the box? Didn't he have some sheep somewhere I could herd? What good was a dog in a box?

Well, I didn't have to wonder long.

One afternoon, a little girl with yellow curls pointed up to me and said, "I want him!"

The girl's father moved on to the beagles. "How about one of these?" he said. "There are lots of nice dogs in this pet shop."

"I want *him*! I want *him*! I want *him*!" the little girl shrieked, jumping up and down.

The father smiled. I guess he liked the way she jumped and shrieked. "Well, it's *your* birthday," he said. "You get to choose!"

The man with all the animals opened my box and lifted me out.

"You are one lucky pup," he said, handing me over to the father. "You're going to have a new home!"

We got into a shiny blue car. Penelope, that was the little girl's name, put me on her lap. I hopped right off to explore that car, but she yanked me back. "You have to sit still," she said. Well, I was so excited I could hardly hold my water much less sit still. But I tried. Penelope wasn't very strong, but she could shriek like anything. The world went flying by that car window so fast I couldn't see straight. Penelope had her arms locked tight around me and I could hardly breathe.

I was glad when at last we came to a stop in front of a big white house. We all got out, and Penelope put me down. I ran straight for the grass. All around the grass were pointy white sticks and red flowers. The flowers poked your nose if you tried to smell them.

I was about to mark my new territory when Penelope snatched me right off my feet and took me into the house.

In no time at all, she had a dress on me with a matching bonnet and was pushing me in a baby stroller.

"You're the baby, Blackie," Penelope said, "and I'm the mommy. Now don't wet your pants, baby, or Mommy will have to spank you!"

It just makes you cringe, doesn't it?

"Oh, honey," said Penelope's mother to Penelope's father, "come see this! Isn't this the cutest thing?"

No help there. My self-respect was leaking like a rusty bucket. At last I was released from my silly clothes and taken outside. There I was given a corner of the yard in which to do my business and a miniature version of the white house to live in.

By myself. Nobody to cuddle with, no warm fur except my own, a rubber bone to chew on.

It was a sorrowful existence for a pup. The glass box had been bad enough, but at least I had company. Sorry to say, I wasn't very brave that first night. I whined and howled my head off, but nobody came. Except for the cat. She cruised by a couple of times, waving the tip of her tail. No sympathy at all. But what can you expect from a cat?

After breakfast—more pellets—I got ready to endure another day as Baby. But, to my relief, Penelope went off in a big yellow bus. Then the father drove away in his blue car, the mother took off in a red car with no roof, and I was left behind. Imprisoned. Held against my will, attached by a chain to a doghouse.

I couldn't stay, of course. You knew that, right? And I knew Penelope would be sad to lose me—she'd never get that cat to play Baby, that's for sure—but I had to get out of there. Life in the pretty white house wasn't life, at least not for a dog like me.

But one last try.

That night when the father came home from work, I tried my best to show him what I was all about. I dodged and feinted, ran full speed around the yard herding imaginary sheep, then stopped on a dime and switched directions. I even tried herding him, but he just didn't get it. He let me play for a while in the yard with Penelope—she couldn't throw a ball worth a darn, though my mom said lots of girls can. Then it was time for dinner. Penelope and Dad went inside. Me? I was supposed to entertain myself.

Doing what? Chasing butterflies?

It was a bad matchup, that's all, me with them. They needed a sit-around dog, a lie-in-your-lap dog, not a sheepherder like me.

It was easy getting out of there once I'd decided to go; the pointy sticks were no higher than the father's knee. One day when I was taken off my chain, instead of playing with Penelope I just hopped over the sticks and took off. Didn't dare look back. I hate to see a kid cry.

I don't know what I thought I was doing. Wasn't thinking, I guess. All I knew was that I'd had a purpose once, a reason for being alive. I'd found it running with the fellas, and if it took the rest of my life, I was going to find it again.

3

I RAN, forever it seemed, past houses like the one I'd escaped. Dogs chained or fenced barked in greeting, or in warning. A porch light came on, and there was my shadow, racing just ahead of me. A man on the porch yelled, "Hey!" I kept on running, away from those big houses and clean streets into the darker end of that town, where my blackness would blend in. There was so much to sniff there that I had to slow down. Cat, rat, paper that smelled like food, dog everywhere. I'd never been so excited, or so scared.

At last I found a corner of a vacant lot to lie down in, my belly knotted with hunger. There I spent a fitful night, no dreams of home to ease my slumber. I'd drop off, then wake up with a start, thinking I'd heard something. A big black truck with a rackety engine, Penelope calling "Blackie! Blackie!," the click of a glass door shutting me in.

Morning came and I hit the streets again, trying my best to look as if I had something to do, a place to go.

I guess I thought if I went far enough, looked hard enough, after a little while, a day or two maybe, I'd find Bob. He'd recognize me by the white spot on the tip of my tail, and he'd see right away that I didn't have a home. What could he do but take me back?

The town was starting to wake itself up, shopkeepers sweeping their sidewalks, bread trucks and milk trucks and meat trucks passing like empty promises. To get my mind off food, I ran alongside a boy delivering newspapers. Until the boy got nosy. "Hey, you're a stray, aren't you?" He stopped his bike, but by the time he'd set that bike down, I was gone.

It was a bacon morning. Out of every window, the delicious odor of pig meat frying. I could hardly stand it. By the time I found breakfast—half a hamburger in a tipped over garbage can—I was so hungry I almost ate the paper it came in. (I didn't tip the can, by the way. I could still imagine the scolding I'd get from Mom if she caught me. I didn't dare think how life would be if I never saw my mom again.)

At every house people were up and going places, getting into cars and going off with big, important things to do. Kids jumped on their bikes or climbed onto school buses, leaving the houses empty and quiet. Or a dog would stay behind to mind things. The cats didn't help. Cats have very little use for people, no matter how they might pretend otherwise. But the dogs always watched the people's every move, afraid they'd never come back.

I made a few friends among the mixed breeds. One let me drink from her personal water bowl. I think she wanted me to stick around, but no way was I going to end up chained to a house again, not in this life.

I sniffed my way across town, then through a big, empty park, and at last ran smack into a highway, cars flying back and forth faster than Old Dex on his best day. I was trying to decide which way to go when I caught the distinct scent of something rank and woolly. I lifted my nose, sniffed again. Sheep? Sheep! The smell, terrible but wonderful for what it promised, drifted toward me. My heart lifted, and I raced in the direction of the smell. Bob! It had to be Bob!

❁

They appeared like a funny kind of dream, a white blur, jingling and jangling like Christmas. The closer they came, the slower I went. These weren't sheep. They *looked* sort of like sheep. They *smelled* sort of like sheep, but they sure weren't sheep. The look in their weird yellow eyes, for one thing. They were harnessed all together in a long line, pulling a wagon with a little red house that sat sort of sideways on top.

"Ho!" said the man walking beside the wagon. "Ho,

you mangy varmints!" The goats came to a jangling stop, snorting and fussing. "Hey, fella," said the man, his hand laid flat so that I could sniff its trustworthiness. I was less careful in those days than I've learned to be, and a lot more lonely. One sniff and I was all over him, telling him my many troubles. "Well, yes," the Goat Man said. "Sure. Danged if it isn't so." Things like that, to let me know he understood.

The Goat Man had the longest beard. Gray and curly, it hung halfway down a ratty old jacket that might have been yellow once. On his head was a floppy brown hat stained with sweat and tied under his chin with string. Between the hat and the beard were eyes the color of the sky above Bob and Ellen's ranch, just as clear and bright blue.

The goats were a whole lot less friendly. They shuffled around impatiently while the Goat Man and I got to know each other. Then while they grazed on the grass alongside the highway, the Goat Man poured me a bowl of goat's milk, thick and tangy. I lapped it up like it came from my mother. "That should hold you for a while," the Goat Man said. "A growing pup needs sustenance."

I figured sustenance was another name for the milk, but he meant more than that. He meant love and hope and that sort of thing. He knew what I needed all right. I needed a home. Watching the Goat Man put away the bowl and the jug of milk, I knew I wanted to stay with him. There were things he could teach me. And I could help with the goats. But would he take me with him? Would he want another hungry belly to feed?

The Goat Man got up from the rock he was resting on. He never rested long.

"On, you huskies!" he cried, and those goats, with only a little bit of grumbling, started moving, pulling that funny red wagon house on its creaky wooden wheels. I followed along, like I'd followed Old Dex, as if I'd always been a part of the team.

"You're a good pup, Shep," the Goat Man said after a while. "I don't know where your folks are or I'd take you there. I guess you'll have to hitch up with us. We've come all the way up from Mexico, and we're headed for Canada. That okay, boy?"

You can bet I told him in every way I could, mostly with my tail, that it was. Mexico? Canada? What did I know?

We traveled right alongside the highway as the cars whizzed by. The Goat Man waved at the people in the cars, and when the children waved back, the Goat Man's eyes would sparkle. I guessed that his mouth was smiling under all that beard. We walked in sunlight as long as it lasted, and then by moonlight when the sun was gone. I got used to the jingling bells after a while, but the goats wouldn't let me anywhere near them.

They'd kick or butt me if I tried to get close. This just made the Goat Man laugh.

That night, my first night on the team, we went a little off the highway to camp. The goats plopped down in the weeds right where they were. Then the Goat Man cooked us some goat's meat—I'll spare you the particulars—over an open fire, turning it on a stick. Did that ever smell good! When the meat was cooked, he shared it between us. It was as if he'd known all along I was coming for dinner.

You were wondering where I slept, right? You were hoping it would be down there by his feet, and you'd be right. For the first time since leaving home, I slept a genuine all-out puppy sleep.

❂

The bells awoke me. The goats were restless, ready to hit the road. It was all they knew. Life was one long, straight run of grass or no grass. Something to be said for the simplicity of that. I found a piece of the Goat Man's face to lick him awake.

"Whoa, Shep! You must be hungry, huh, fella?" He pushed the door of the wagon house open. I hopped out and did my business. We had our breakfast, milk for me, cheese and milk for him. Then we began moving again. Early, it wasn't so bad, a few cars, the air still smelling like it was meant to. After a while, I didn't know which was worse, the goats or the cars. If I hadn't loved the Goat Man so much, I don't think I could have hung on as long as I did. A long time in people years, even longer in dog years.

Why we stuck to the highway was a mystery to me. All that exhaust and the smell of burned rubber when he could have gone into the hills. After I got to know the Goat Man better, I began to figure it out. The highway was just part of the bigger thing he believed in, his place on the earth. Never asked for a thing, the Goat Man. I never once saw him reach his hand out for someone else's money. It would never have occurred to him to beg. He had all he needed. Goat's milk and the cheese he made from it, some goat's meat now and then, and his wisdom. Cropping the grass wherever it grew was the Goat Man's purpose, his payment for the little space on the earth he and the goats took up. The circle of life, he called it.

Most nights, after we'd stopped and had our dinner, while the goats grazed, the Goat Man would get to work on what he called his Words of Wisdom cards. "Now that's a good one!" he'd say, scratching his chin somewhere under all that beard. "Listen to this one, Shep!" I'd cock my head, and he'd read me what he wrote. I guessed it was wisdom, though I really didn't know. Most cards he decorated with pictures. Well, sort of pictures. He was better with the words. When he was finished, he put a rubber band around the cards.

"Wisdom," he said, with that little wink he always gave me. "That's what people need right now, and I'm just the person to give them some. Well, me and President Eisenhower."

Then he'd curl up under his pile of quilts, and in no time at all he'd be snoring.

It wasn't an exciting life. I had a higher calling, and I knew it. But I loved the Goat Man. He taught me all I knew. Not about the sheep—Dad and Old Dex taught me that. But about philosophy, which is just a big word for big ideas. Like what things mean, and how to live the best life.

Trouble was, sometimes the philosophy would happen at the very worst times, when I was tired and hungry and had to whine a little to get the Goat Man's attention. Like once after a real long day, when we were camped for the night and the Goat Man was fixing our dinner. He'd put some goat's meat on to cook, and my nose was as close to that meat as it could be without setting my fur on fire. "Shep," the Goat Man said, and I knew by the sound of his voice that the philosophy was coming. "You will journey far and wide if you make your sails of patience."

See what I mean? Sails of patience? It took some doing to understand the Goat Man's meaning sometimes, and by then the meat was ready.

Worse was when the Goat Man came up with something so good he'd have to write it on a card right then. Our meat would shrink to nothing and turn black as coal.

The Goat Man would always be sorry he'd ruined our dinner, but not for long. "Don't cry over spilled goat's milk," he'd say, chuckling to himself.

I never did get it.

4

WINTERS WERE HARD, especially for the goats, who needed their grass, but we never stopped traveling. The Goat Man would wear holes right through his boots, repairing them as best he could with cardboard or tying them on with string. It was funny how a new pair would always turn up just in the nick of time, and they'd always fit. People loved the Goat Man. He was doing what they would have liked to do, living in the open air, going where his mood took him.

If it snowed, we'd shelter in a barn or under a canopy of trees. On warmer days, we'd find a stream and nap in the middle of the day. In the evening, when we'd settled ourselves at a campsite and had our dinner, the Goat Man would read us poetry by the light of the fire, or play some tunes. I liked the sound of the poetry all right, but that accordion hurt my ears. "If music be the food of love, play on!" the Goat Man said. "That's Shakespeare, Shep. He was pretty handy with words of wisdom, too."

Nights were always the best. Even if it rained, I was

right there next to my best friend, all snuggled up inside the little wagon house as the rain danced on our roof.

A good many dog years passed that way. I had been growing into a "right handsome beast" is how the Goat Man put it.

❂

It was sometime during our last year together, though neither of us knew it. We were in a place called Oregon, the Goat Man said, and the air had begun to cool. He was selling his Words of Wisdom cards the way he always did in the winter. He'd sell them wherever he could, hoarding the few coins he got to buy hay for the goats. And every now and then, a meaty bone for me, even though I didn't earn my keep. Oh, I ran alongside the goats, keeping them in line. But they didn't need much herding. They'd gotten along fine without me. Still, I had to practice my skills.

The Goat Man was older than I knew, people years were a mystery to me then. Toward the end of that long, cold winter, the Goat Man took sick. For some time we didn't travel, lying low behind an abandoned barn while the Goat Man slept. One night, as I lay warming his feet, he woke up and, as if he were still in a dream, began talking about Trudy. She must have been a real special person the way the Goat Man went on and on about her. But her father didn't like the Goat Man (who wasn't the Goat Man yet, just an ordinary farm boy). He wanted his pretty daughter to marry the son of a wealthy farmer. No amount of begging and crying was going to turn the father's cold heart away from that plan. The wealthy farmer's money was going to save their poor farm, and that was that.

They were so in love, the Goat Man said, that there was no help for it: they had to be together. One night, with only a slice of the moon to see by, the Goat Man came with a ladder and set it up under Trudy's bedroom window. The two took off to the next county and married.

How the Goat Man chuckled telling the story of the big escape. But then he began to cough and cough. After a while, he slept. Toward morning, when the goats were starting to rustle and snort, he picked up the story again.

This part was so sad, I wished I'd slept through it.

They made a good life for themselves, young as they were. Trudy took in washing, the Goat Man worked a neighboring farm. In the spring, when Trudy said they'd be adding a child to their family, he was happier than he'd ever been in his life. "True love is a banquet for the soul," the Goat Man said. But the birth was a hard one, not your usual thing, and when Trudy and their newborn son passed away shortly afterward, the Goat Man, who was not yet a goat man, became one. He left that little place with all the goats they had and never looked back.

"Love and grief grow in the same garden," the Goat Man said.

Later that morning we went back to the highway, but the Goat Man had slowed down some. We had to keep stopping so that he could catch his breath. After a while, he climbed up into his little house and left things to me. Well, the goats and I, we had our routine. Nobody to wave to the kids in the cars, nobody selling Words of Wisdom, but we kept on moving.

And then one morning my tongue didn't work the way it always had: I licked the Goat Man's face, the part I could get to, but his eyes wouldn't open. I yipped a couple of times—you know the yip, kind of sharp and high in the throat. But the Goat Man didn't move. I nosed open the door and went out to reassure the goats, acting all businesslike, running up and down the line. The goats looked me over with their little yellow eyes as if to say, "Who do you think you are anyway? You're not the boss of us."

They were right. But I didn't know what else to do. We had to go on. It was all we knew.

With some badgering, the goats got themselves up and into a line more or less. They were skittish, kept waiting for the Goat Man's "On, you huskies!" I nipped a few heels out of desperation, and at last we began to move.

I didn't know how to stop them was the thing. I could make them move all right, but they didn't have any brakes. I kept wanting to stop so that I could check on the Goat Man, see if he was awake yet. But the goats kept on going. That's the thing about goats and sheep. Some children, too, if you want the truth. If you don't set your fence out there somewhere, they'll just keep going with never a thought. Get themselves into all kinds of trouble.

It was dark by the time the goats wore out. They had some way of talking, I never could figure out how. But suddenly they stopped. Like they were all one animal. They stopped on the side of the road and plopped down.

Well.

I went running back to the wagon. I knew the Goat Man would be real hungry by then. I sure was. He'd be unwrapping the cheese, pouring us our milk. I yipped at the door to the wagon house, but the Goat Man didn't answer. It was harder to open the door from the outside, but at last it fell open. I hopped inside and onto his bed.

Nothing had changed. The Goat Man was going to sleep forever. I lay down beside him then, not at his feet, where I belonged, but right up next to his dear old face. If he opened his eyes, I was going to be right there to say hello.

Well, of course, by now you know he never did.

We went on like that for another long day. Didn't know what else to do, neither the goats nor me, a caravan of lost souls. I knew something had to be done, but the goats surely weren't going to do it. Things were working pretty much the way they always had for them. Grass, no grass. I was the one having the hard time of it. I'd lost my best friend. No way did I need a bunch of nasty goats.

Toward the end of that second day, I spotted a small barn with a house beside it. A farmer was driving a tractor through a big empty field, the earth turning in dark waves behind him. There was wash on the line, a tire swing hanging from a tree. Here were people who could use some goats, said I. Running and feinting and dodging and sweeping, I herded those goats straight into the field. They were so surprised they didn't have time to complain. They went like sheep.

The farmer came riding back on his tractor and stopped. Took off his hat, scratched his head. "Well, what have we here?" he said. I hoped he wasn't as dumb as that. Anybody could see that what we had here was a sorry herd of goats and a broken-down wagon.

All things considered, I suppose I should have stayed. But the farmer had no sheep, and I was real tired of those goats. After a good meal, thanks to the farmer's wife, I headed out across the land. If I never saw another highway, well, that was fine with me.

But first I had to say goodbye to the Goat Man. I hopped up into the wagon house, and there he was, just as I'd left him. I sniffed his curly beard, his closed eyes, his rough old hand. Storing him up for memory was what I was doing, though I didn't know it then.

After a while, I hopped down and headed off, the way the Goat Man left Trudy. Not because I wanted to, but because it was all there was left to do. I stopped just once, turned back, and saw the farmer climbing into the wagon.

5

LIFE WAS EASIER without the goats. I could travel faster, go where my nose took me, get away from that highway. But it wasn't easy for long.

That first day on my own I stopped in at a few farms, poked around looking for some lunch, too proud to beg. Scared a chicken off her nest and grabbed an egg. Smashed the thing in my mouth. It took me forever to lick the shell off. Sticky darn thing an egg is. Weak with hunger, I went along a dirt road, then a paved road, and came at last to a town.

It wasn't much of a town. There were just a couple of streets. One street went straight down to the water. At the water's edge, men unloaded nets filled with silvery things into big wooden boxes. Curiosity and hunger made me brave. I went to investigate.

The men paid no attention to me, they had their work to do. They were big and loud and laughed a lot. In their thick rubber boots and yellow slickers, they slogged through puddles cold enough to make me shiver. I hung back as long as I could, but I had to see what was in those boxes.

It was sort of like the difference between sheep and goats. The stuff in the boxes didn't *look* like food, but it *smelled* like food. One box had a bunch of spiny red things with mean-looking pinchers on their paws. I left them alone. Another box had slimy silver things piled to the top. I sniffed the side of a silvery thing with a dead, staring eye. It reminded me of the creatures in the pet shop, only a whole lot bigger.

"Hey, whatcha doin' there? You a fish dog?"

I looked up, ready to bolt, but the fisherman was dog people, you could tell right away. He knelt and gave me a nice rubdown.

I had to get back to that fish.

"You want some cod, is that it? Okay, here you go." The fisherman grabbed the very fish I'd been sniffing and slapped it down on the dock. Then with a sharp knife he slit that thing right up the middle. Out came all this squishy stuff. Off came the skin. The fisherman laid a piece of white fish meat on his palm and held it out to me. I sniffed it, not bad. So I gobbled it up. The fisherman laughed while I ate the rest of that fish meat. "This here's a fish dog!" he said to the others. "Ever see a dog who liked fish this much?"

Well, I was hungry is all. I'd have eaten the red spiny things if that's all there was.

Back on the road, I lived on that fish for a couple of days, don't know how I held out. Proud, I guess. I'd seen the skinny homeless dogs that roamed the streets in search of garbage. Strays. But I wasn't one of them. I wasn't a stray. I was a Border collie of distinctive lineage in search of employment. They knew it, too. "Oh, so you're too good for us, huh?" their eyes would say. "Well, just you wait."

They were right, of course. Life on the open road was a brave adventure, but only if your belly was full. Then you had the strength to explore, to go any old place your feet and your curiosity could take you. But if you were hungry, life was just a search for food. You couldn't think about anything else. You couldn't enjoy a good romp with a pal you met along the way, or play tag with the kids in the park, or savor all the rich odors of the great outdoors. Your nose had a single purpose, and that was to find food. After a while it didn't even matter what kind.

By the third day after my fish, I found myself down by the railroad tracks. I'd had enough of being chased away from the places where food smell was the most enticing: kitchens, restaurants, family picnics. I'd been hanging around people, acting all pitiful. After a while, it wasn't an act. "Shoo!" the people would say, flapping their arms. "Shoo!" At first I didn't understand. I thought they meant the things they wore on their feet. The Goat Man worried about shoes all the time.

"You're lucky, Shep," he said one time. "You got them permanent kind." Well, my permanent shoes were getting awfully weary. But my belly wouldn't let them rest.

I don't know what I expected to find down by the tracks, but except for crickets, at least it was quiet. And there weren't any people to shoo me on. I nosed my way along the wooden part. Things had died there. Things that once had fur lay smashed and drying in the sun.

My first thought when I heard the train whistle was of my mom and dad. I guess because it's lonely that sound, downright mournful. And then I saw the train approaching, pulling its many cars, blowing clouds into a gray sky. Then the whistle again, the chug-chugging of that big engine, and the train went screaming by.

I trotted alongside the tracks until I heard people talk. I wasn't in the mood for humans, but humans had all the food. Unless you were willing to kill, and I wasn't, you had no choice but to beg. You could act like you didn't care whether or not they shared their food, or you could try to charm them out of it. It came down to the same thing: begging. The Goat Man wouldn't have done it, I knew that. But then he had all the goats.

Two raggedy-looking men were sitting on a log in the middle of a weed patch. One was small and skinny, the other was big as a horse. As soon as he saw me, the big one yelled, "Look, Snatch! A dog!"

The skinny one was busy pushing a threaded needle through a shoe, just like the Goat Man used to do when his shoes fell apart. "Quit cher hollerin'," he muttered.

"It's a doggie! It's a doggie!" yelled the big one. He got up and came lumbering out of the weeds toward me, his arms outstretched. I let him beat on me a little. Well, it was his idea of petting. He got down on one knee and started pounding me with those big old hands. He smelled pretty awful. But he smelled like chicken, too, fried chicken. I was so hungry I licked the grease off his chin.

"Good doggie, nice doggie! Hey, Snatch! Can we keep him? Can we keep this doggie?"

Snatch's eyes were real tired-looking, red-rimmed and watery. He looked at the two of us and shook his head. "Quit hollerin'."

"Okay, okay, Snatch," the big guy whispered. Even his whisper was big. "Can we keep him then?"

"Come over here and try this on," Snatch said. He laid the old black shoe on the ground. The big guy got up. That's when I got a good look at what had stunk so bad, his feet. He stuck a big bare foot into the shoe and headed back toward me.

"Ain'tcha gonna put the other one on?"

"Huh? Oh! Yeah." He shoved his other foot into the other shoe. "He can help us, Snatch," he said. "The doggie can help us, you know, when we get the stuff from the store!" The big guy yelled all the time, even when he tried not to. It made the one called Snatch squinch up his face every time.

Snatch took a good, hard look at me, scratching his whiskery chin. I wagged my tail and cocked my head in the way people seemed to take to. "Looks hungry to me," Snatch said. "What we gonna feed him?"

"He can eat my food!"

"Quit cher hollerin'!"

The big guy, Hollerin I guessed his name was, dug into a cloth bag and pulled out a hunk of chicken. "Here, doggie!" he yelled.

"What d'ya think yer doin'?" It was Snatch who was doing the yelling now. "D'ya think chickens grow on trees?"

That didn't make a whole lot of sense to me. Not to Hollerin either by the look on his face.

"Aw, fugget it," Snatch said. "Where's that cigar we was smoking yestiday?"

Hollerin dug into his bag again. Out came an old brown chewed-up-looking thing that he passed over to Snatch. Snatch stuck it between his lips. Then he struck a match, touched the end of the cigar with it, and sucked some air in. Did that thing ever stink! Worse than Hollerin's bare feet. Snatch began to cough and cough. Then he passed the cigar over to Hollerin.

Well, I'd watched people smoke cigarettes before. Cigars were more or less the same, only the coughing was worse. The Goat Man said he could never understand why people smoked, but I did. It was to make the clouds. They'd get this dreamy look in their eyes sometimes as the smoke rose up, and that's how you could tell. Still, it was strange. The Goat Man said it was like taking poison, and he was never wrong.

After they finished smoking and choking, Snatch and Hollerin spread some coats on the ground and lay down. So I did, too. By the smell of it, Hollerin's pack still had food in it. I was going to stick close and see if he would give me more.

After a while, Hollerin sat up and stretched. "Let's get a chocolate milk shake!" he yelled.

"Can'tcha let a guy sleep?" Snatch rolled over. Then he got up and peed in the bushes. Hollerin' did, too, marking the place for later, so nobody else would take it.

Hollerin kept on and on about the milk shake, and Snatch kept telling him to shut up. After a while Snatch gave in. "Okay! Okay! Lemme see how much money we got."

He dug into his pocket and came out with some paper money and some coins. "This is it," he said. "It's all we got left."

Hollerin hung down over Snatch's hand. "Enough for a chocolate milk shake?"

Snatch frowned at the little pile of money. "It is," he

said, "if we don't buy any supper. But you don't care about that, right?"

"I don't care about supper," Hollerin yelled, shaking his big head. "I just want a chocolate milk shake!"

"You just want a chocolate milk shake," Snatch said. He sighed and stuffed the money back into his pocket. "Aw right, come on then." He slung his pack over his shoulder, and Hollerin did the same. I think he forgot all about me then, but I trotted along behind him, keeping an eye on that pack.

It was a long walk for that milk shake, and Hollerin never stopped yelling about it until we got to the place where they made them. Then he slurped it down so fast.

"I hope yer satisfied," Snatch muttered. "We gotta get us some stuff for supper now. You ready?"

"I'm ready," Hollerin said. Then his big, soft-looking eyes got wide. "And the doggie's ready, too. Aren't you, doggie?"

"Might as well name the mutt," Snatch said. "Ya can't keep callin' him doggie. People won't believe he's yers. They'll think somethin's fishy. Then what? Didja think about that?"

Hollerin's mouth hung open while he thought about that. "Spot," he said after a while. "That's what I'm going to name him."

"Now where didja ever get that name?" Snatch said.

He began to laugh and cough, pounding his skinny chest with his fist.

" 'Cause he's got this spot!" Hollerin yelled. "He's got this big white spot on his tail."

"Well, ain'tcha one smart fellow," Snatch said.

6

I FOLLOWED SNATCH and Hollerin down the main
street. All the shops were open, people going in and
coming out.

A pretty little spaniel caught my eye. She was on a
leash but didn't seem to mind. She walked ahead of
her mistress with such an air of self-possession that
you wondered who was walking whom. The spaniel
stopped to give me a good sniff of her. I let her do the
same. We touched noses, and I went back for another
sniff.

"Come, Phoebe!" her mistress said, giving the spaniel's
leash a tug. We said a reluctant goodbye, and I watched
her go off, her head and tail high.

And then I remembered: Snatch and Hollerin!
Where were they? I ran up the street, dodging legs and
bicycles, poking my nose into shop doors. They were
nowhere to be found. In just the few minutes that I'd
let myself be a real dog, I'd lost them.

I stopped in the middle of the sidewalk as the people
went walking by, feeling strange inside, a little sick and

a whole lot sad. I guess it was a sign of how much I'd come to depend on the Goat Man's company. I needed a home, I needed some folks. My life on the road as an independent dog was only a couple of days old, and I'd already had enough of it.

Just then I heard a great commotion. People were slowing down to watch something going on across the street. I found my way clear of the legs, and what do you know—it was Snatch and Hollerin. I raced across the street to join them, but they had their hands full and didn't see me.

Snatch was loaded down with bread and bananas. Hollerin had a jug of milk and a whole wheel of cheese. A man was yelling, "Stop, thieves!" and swatting Snatch on the head with a newspaper.

"Run!" Snatch yelled.

It took Hollerin a little time to get that big body moving. Then the two of them were racing side by side down the street, dodging cars and people, and I went racing after them.

"Whole lotta good your doggie did us!" Snatch said when we were back in the weeds again.

Hollerin gave me the saddest look. "Don't feel bad," he said. "He don't want to say mean things. It's just how he is."

"Slice us off some of that cheese," Snatch said. "You didn't have to grab the whole blasted thing, you know.

How's a guy supposed to live on cheese? Milk and cheese and bananas. We gotta do better than this."

Well, the Goat Man did just fine on milk and cheese, but I couldn't tell Snatch that. Snatch was one of those people who didn't listen much anyway. He mostly did the talking and deciding, while Hollerin did the listening and the yelling. They were a team that way.

I missed the Goat Man so much that night, lying beside Hollerin, the sky spread over us with its blanket of stars. I guessed I'd found a new home. It wasn't much, a patch of weeds was all, but as you well know, a home isn't just the stuff it's made out of. As a cold wind crept into our camp, I snuggled closer to Hollerin, who was just as warm as he was big.

The next day and the next I had nothing to eat but the milk Hollerin gave me, mixed in with a little bread. He laid some banana on the ground for me, too, and when I didn't touch it, he picked it up and popped it in his mouth.

"I'm tired of this damned cheese!" Snatch said on the fourth day. "We need to get us some money. Buy some proper food, like proper people, in a market."

"Yeah!" yelled Hollerin.

"Well, get up then. Ain't gonna do it by myself."

"Spot's coming, too," Hollerin said. "Aren't you, Spot? You're going to help us today. Right, Snatch? He's gonna help us, right?"

Snatch stopped what he was doing, and I watched an idea hatch in his eyes. "Well, I'll be," he said. "If that pea brain of yours didn't come up with something useful for a change! Listen up now. I'll tell you what we'll do."

"Okay, Snatch, okay! I'm listening."

"Then quitcher hollerin' and listen."

Snatch grabbed on to Hollerin's arm while he explained what he had in mind, I guess so's Hollerin wouldn't wander off. When he was finished, Hollerin turned to me.

"You have to play dead now," he said.

When I didn't do what he said—I didn't know how—he got down on the ground and showed me. Hollerin with all four feet in the air and his eyes squeezed shut was something to see. Snatch laughed so hard he had to slap his knees to calm down.

"Okay, now you," Hollerin said, lumbering to his feet.

It was easy enough. I lay down, rolled over, stuck my paws in the air, and closed my eyes.

Hollerin clapped and cheered.

"If you two ain't an act," Snatch said.

They walked ahead, going in a different direction than the day before, Snatch talking to Hollerin while I snuffled through the weeds thinking about gophers and field mice. Their homes were everywhere. Could I eat one if I had to? If I caught one, how was I supposed to

46

kill it? Bite its head off? The whole thing was enough to make me a vegetarian. Besides, I wasn't about to take my eyes off Snatch and Hollerin and lose them again.

We weren't in town five minutes before Hollerin said to play dead. The sidewalk was hard, but I did it anyway. Then Hollerin dropped to his knees and started wailing. "My doggie! My doggie! My doggie's dead! Help! Help!"

People began to gather around. My eyes were shut, but I could hear them.

"What's going on here? What's the matter with your dog?"

"Oh, he's all right! Can't you see he's just playing dead?"

"No, he isn't! What's the matter with you? That dog needs medical attention. Don't worry, big fellow. We'll call somebody!"

After a while, I'd had enough of that. I opened my eyes and hopped up.

"He's all better!" Hollerin yelled.

"See? What did I tell you?" a man said to his wife. "He was just playing dead."

"Good doggie! Good boy, Spot!" said Hollerin. "I'll tell Snatch to buy you a treat!"

Where was Snatch? We walked along the street for a while, Hollerin looking everywhere for Snatch. Then there he was, just like that, walking beside us.

"Snatch!" Hollerin yelled, as if he hadn't seen his friend in weeks. "How did Spot and me do?"

"You did fine, fine!" Snatch hissed. "Now shut up or we'll end up in the hoosegow."

Wherever that was, Hollerin didn't want to go there. He whispered all the way back to camp. As soon as we got there, Snatch began pulling wallets out of his pockets and dropping them on the ground. Then he knelt down and started going through them. "Good take," he said.

"It was because of Spot!" Hollerin said. "The people never saw what you were doing!"

"Yeah, yeah, Spot's a real hero! I'm just the one did the dirty work."

✦

The weather grew colder, but still we stayed in our weed camp. It wasn't much of a home, but it was all we had. One morning we awoke with snow covering us like a thin white quilt.

Snatch jumped up and shook himself off. "Time to head south," he said.

"Let's go to California!" Hollerin yelled. "The snow's not so cold in California!"

California? My ears went right up. California was home. Home and Bob, Mom and Dad.

"Ain't no snow in California, you idjit. Find some sticks," Snatch said. "I'll make us a fire."

Hollerin and I went in search of something to burn. There wasn't much.

While the snow fell, we sat around that meager fire warming our paws and noses. "We'll be froze before the Southbound comes," Snatch said, rubbing his hands over the flames.

"Not Spot," Hollerin said. "He's got a good warm coat on him. Maybe California's too warm for Spot."

"Don't you worry none about Spot," Snatch said.

The snow stopped after a while and the sun came out. Snatch got up and stretched. "Time to get on down the road," he said. "Southbound train's due any time now."

"Oh, boy!" Hollerin said. "California!"

California! We were going to California. I gave a little woof of joy and Hollerin laughed.

"Make sure you pack all your stuff," Snatch said. "You leave it, you don't see it never again."

Hollerin started packing his things. He didn't have much. "Spot's lucky," he said. "He doesn't need to carry one thing."

"Spot's a dog, dummy," Snatch said.

"I know that," Hollerin said. "I know that, Snatch."

We set out in the opposite direction from town, walking alongside the tracks. What little sun there was felt warm and good on my back.

"Okay, this is where we wait," Snatch said. "Down here."

We went down the bank to a flat place. Snatch and Hollerin knelt in the bushes. I dozed off. Chicken legs raced back and forth through my dreams. When I heard the train whistle, I woke right up. Snatch and Hollerin jumped to their feet. The train was coming toward us, chuffing and steaming, slowing way down to round the bend.

"That one!" yelled Snatch, pointing at the train. "That car, see it? The red one!"

"I see it, Snatch!" yelled Hollerin.

"Then go! Go!" cried Snatch, and Hollerin climbed up that bank as fast as his big body would go, his arms flapping like he was trying to fly. I took off, too. Or tried to. But I was caught in the bushes.

"So long, doggie," Snatch said. That's when I saw that I was tied. Looped around my neck was a length of thick brown rope. I barked, but Hollerin had already dived through the open door of the red train car. He held out his hand for Snatch to leap up, and then they were both inside.

The train began to gather speed. I saw Hollerin lean out the door, so far he almost fell. "Spot!" he cried. "Spot! Come on! Come on! We're going to California!"

7

IT TOOK ME a while to chew through that rope, and when I was finished I had a noose around my neck. I lay down in the bushes, feeling pretty low. Hollerin was right, I said to myself, California would have been too warm for me. I wouldn't have liked it much. But that was just to make me feel better. I told myself that lots of folks would want a dog like me. Mostly, I tried to tell myself that I was fine. I'd been on my own before. Never for long, but I could make it.

The thing is, I'd been tricked. That was the worst part. Snatch didn't have to trick me. He could have explained in a reasonable way that a dog just wasn't in the plans. Another mouth to feed, all that kind of stuff. Then Hollerin and I, we could have said a proper good-bye.

But Hollerin wouldn't have been reasonable. Love isn't always reasonable. He'd have fought to keep me, and Snatch would have given in. He always did. Snatch took care of things the only way he knew how, with trickery. That's the kind of person he was. But he cared about Hollerin, too, and so he wasn't all bad. He just didn't give himself a chance to know me, that's all.

Anyway, that's what I told myself.

I spent the night there in the bushes, cold and shivering. I'd grown used to Hollerin, even his smell. In the middle of the night, whenever a cold wind came up, he was warm as a pile of pups.

In the morning, I headed back into town to beg for my breakfast. Begging wasn't exactly noble or even honorable, but it was better than stealing. I never did feel good about my part in Snatch's schemes. Food bought with stolen money didn't taste right, at least to me it didn't.

It was a sorry day for beggars. Maybe it was the cold, but nobody was willing to part with as much as a crust of bread. Not that I was hoping for bread. I was hanging around the back of a butcher shop when wham! I was caught again. Tangled up in my paws, tying me in knots, was a fishnet!

Or anyway, that's what it looked like.

"Hold him!" somebody yelled, and a hand pushed my head to the ground. I yelped, and bit at the net. What was happening to me? I tried a pitiful whine, but that didn't work. Before I knew it I'd been thrown into a metal box I couldn't even turn around in. I felt the rumble of an engine in my stomach and the whir of tires. I scratched at the metal door. I yelped and whined. Even though I knew it wouldn't do any good, I couldn't seem to stop myself. All I could think of was that awful day when I'd been taken from my parents.

"Oh, shut up for heaven's sake!"

A yelp stuck in my throat, and I coughed. "What?"

The voice came from the other side of my metal box. "Relax! It's only a short ride. You don't have to carry on like you're being murdered."

"Where are we going?" I didn't want to go back to the pet store. What if Penelope found me there and took me home again? Hard as my life was on the road, it was a whole lot better than being the baby. "Where are we going?" I asked again.

"The pound. Where did you think?"

We made a couple more stops. I heard dogs yipping, fighting their fate. But they all ended up in the truck. You never heard such a racket as we dogs made going down the road. I joined right in, of course. Misery loves company, like the Goat Man used to say.

"Will yez all shut up?"

But we drowned that voice right out.

I thought we'd go on forever. My throat was sore from barking and my legs cramped from being in such a tight space, so I was glad when the truck came to a stop. One by one our boxes were opened and we were hauled into pens inside a long, gray building.

The howling inside that truck was nothing compared

to what was going on in there, dogs in rows of cages all begging to be set free. Dogs of every breed, color, and size, all yapping their fool heads off.

"That's the worst part about this place," the voice said, "all the blasted noise."

I turned and saw the sheepdog in the cage next to mine who had been only a voice before. He couldn't see me, though. Or at least I thought he couldn't for all the hair in his eyes.

"Where are we?" I asked.

"You never been here? It's the pound. Don't know why they call it that. They don't pound us on the head or nothin'."

"Do we have to stay here?" I was shaking all over from fear but trying not to show it.

The sheepdog just looked at me, or didn't look at me. Well, you know what I mean. "Depends," he said.

"Huh?"

"You're young, you'll go quick."

"Go? Where?"

"Give you a tip," he said, "then I'm going to sack out for a while."

I cocked my ears and waited. This guy had been around a lot longer than I had. He knew things.

"When the people come, don't get all wild, that's all. Don't do what the rest of these jerks do. Don't holler and beg and all that. Behave yourself. Be patient. Look smart."

He had to know how smart I was. I'm a Border collie, after all. He was only a sheepdog, and probably a lazy one by the looks of him. But I appreciated his advice and told him so.

"Don't mention it," he said.

"Do you know about the sheep?" I asked him. "Where they keep all the sheep?"

"Sheep? What's that?"

A sheepdog that didn't know sheep? I couldn't believe it.

"Well," I began, trying my best to explain, "they're fat and real slow and they're covered with this wool . . ."

I could see he didn't get it. "No sheep here," he said. "Dogs is all."

"But out there," I persisted. "Out there in the fields. Did you ever see a flock of sheep and Bob on his horse and—"

"Don't know no Bob," he said.

My mind had always known how far we were from Bob, but my heart never wanted to get it.

"Time for a snooze," the sheepdog said. He padded to the back of his cage and thumped himself down like a big furry rug.

I tried making friends with the mixed breed on the other side, but she only wanted to complain about "the accommodations," whatever that was.

After a while, all the dogs but me settled down. They slept or hunted for fleas, biting their sore backsides.

I was bored. That's the thing about Border collies. We've got to have something to do, something to keep our minds busy. And there was nothing in that cage. Nothing to chew on, nothing to nose around or chase, not even a bug. I ran in circles for a while, my nails clicking on the concrete floor. I had to get out of that cage. Somehow. I knew I'd go crazy if I had to stay in there long.

Well, I ran myself ragged. Then I plopped down and fell into an exhausted sleep, the floor cold and hard beneath me.

In no time, or some time, I don't know which, the place was a madhouse again, dogs barking, yipping, whining, throwing themselves against their doors.

One by one, metal bowls scraped across the floor into our cages. It was that paper-bag food again, like the stuff at the pet store, but you can bet on an empty stomach it tasted like real food.

That night in my dreams I ran with the sheep for the very first time. It was like a gift, that dream. I could smell the grass again, bump my nose against the woolly side of a fat sheep, hear Bob call from across that moving gray sea. I was quick as an eye blink when he called, darted this way and that way, dodged and feinted. My paws felt sure and strong beneath me.

"Good job, son," I heard Dad say.

I awoke with his voice still in my head. *Good job,*

son. I knew that's what my dad would have said to me in time. I saw the pride in his eyes as he watched me try my best to herd those sheep. He was waiting for me to learn, to grow into my craft. He thought there was time.

❂

The next day, and all the days after, whenever the people came, I was on my best behavior. While the other dogs carried on, I did what the sheepdog said. I sat with my head erect, my tail wagging an invitation.

Some people had come to find the dogs they'd lost. What happiness when they were reunited! Kisses, slobber. It made my heart hurt. But I didn't let it show. I waited patiently for somebody to notice me. Sometimes they did.

"Let's get that one!" a boy or girl would say, stopping at my cage. The kids liked me. But the moms or dads didn't for some reason. They'd say I wasn't a house dog (they were right about that!). They'd worry about having to walk me every day. One mom looked at me as if she was about to change her mind. Then she said, "There's something wrong with him. I don't know . . . He's too *perfect.*"

Days passed, and I was getting desperate. I had to get out of that cage, I had to find the sheep. I'd plead with my eyes, my tail. I'd even started to whine a little.

One day, when I thought everybody had gone, I began complaining to the sheepdog. "Nobody ever picks me. I'll never get out of here!"

"You're trying too hard," the sheepdog said. "Relax!"

That was when I noticed the man hanging back by the wall, leaning against it, picking his yellow teeth with a little stick, looking at me from under bushy black eyebrows.

My tail stopped wagging, and a feeling like cold metal came into my heart.

"This one," the man said after a while, pointing straight at me.

The door opened, and a lady leaned in. She was the one who fed us and had cut the rope from my neck, so I trusted her. "Come on," she said. "Come on out now."

Out was what I wanted. It was a stronger feeling than fear, that need to be free of the cage.

"We'll put this on him," the man said. He leaned over me, and before I knew what was happening, I was wearing my first collar. It was awful, a wide leather thing that weighed my neck down. But the worst part was the muzzle, a cage for my mouth. I tried to shake it off, but it was on to stay.

"He's pretty well behaved," the woman said. I don't think she liked the looks of that muzzle either. "These dogs are smart as a rule."

"I know their kind. Too smart for their own good." The man's laugh wasn't like any I'd heard before or since. It had a crack in it, like it was broken, and he always coughed up something afterward and spit it on the ground. "He'll be some trouble all right, but he'll learn."

"He'll need a place to run," the woman said. "Your Border collie can cause some trouble if he's not kept busy."

The man laughed that wicked laugh again. "Oh, he'll be busy all right."

Busy. That sounded good to me. He had a beard like the Goat Man's and a belly like the Goat Man's, and I figured, well, maybe he had some goats like the Goat Man. I went without a fight.

Not that I had a choice. Once we were outside and the door had closed behind us, a chain got attached to my leather collar. "Heel!" the man said.

Heel? What did that mean? I pulled away, dancing back and forth, trying to shake that chain, shake off that awful muzzle.

The first time he hit me with the chain, I was too shocked to feel it. I froze. Something was wrong. I was supposed to understand something, how to do something, how to "heel," but I didn't. I didn't understand. I hung back. Down came that chain again. I yelped. My back stung like it was on fire.

"I said *heel*!" he thundered. Grabbing hold of the

collar, he yanked me alongside, next to his legs. The collar choked me half to death. I stumbled along. By the time he let me go, I'd gotten the idea.

I was on my way to Billy's Big and Happy Circus. Don't let the name fool you.

8

BILLY'S BIG AND HAPPY CIRCUS looked cheery
enough on the outside. But there was only the one tent,
so it wasn't very big, and it sure wasn't happy. Billy led
me at his heel in one flapping door and out the other. I
saw stacked-up chairs, swings hanging down over a
big, wide fishnet. We walked through a mud puddle to
an old gray barn. Billy opened a side door, and I followed him in. It was so dark in there I couldn't see anything at first, not even with my great night vision, but
the stench was awful, so awful I can hardly describe it.
And fear. The smell of fear hung in the air. I shivered all
over.

Billy struck a match, and up loomed the cages, the
sad and angry eyes, the animals, big and small. They
were quiet, which is almost worse than the noise they
could make when they wanted to. They stood in the
gloomy light of the match like the stuff of nightmares.
Then the match went out and I heard a cage door open.
Billy gave me a push, and I was jailed once again.

My eyes were used to the dark by then. My cage—all

the dogs' cages—was more like a chicken coop than like the sturdy one at the pound. But it was strong enough. You couldn't chew your way out, that's for sure.

There were yips of welcome from a couple of terriers in the next cage. I touched noses with them through the wire. They wanted to know all about me, where I'd come from, how I'd gotten caught. Mostly they wanted to know about life on the outside. The terrier brothers —you couldn't tell them apart until you got to know them—had been with Billy all their lives.

"He's not so bad if you don't cross him," said the one Billy called You.

"Just do what he says and you'll be all right," said You Too. He turned to his brother. "Tell him what happened to the other one."

"Sparky? No way, you tell him."

"The whole thing stinks," said You, "and that's the truth."

They argued back and forth about who would tell me what happened to Sparky, whoever he was. Always arguing, those terriers.

"Will you two please, *please* be quiet. I am so tired of your bickering!"

That's when I got my first look at Tiffany.

Love is a funny thing, you know. Not that it's a thing, and not that it's only one kind of thing. There are many kinds of love. But I was young and just beginning to understand how many. Mom and Dad love, Goat Man love, Bob and Ellen love—they were all different. But Tiffany? Well, this was something I'd never felt before. One look at her long, elegant nose, her soft, brown eyes and I felt warm all over, kind of shivery and silly. Only later did I begin to get the whole picture. It wouldn't have mattered what Tiffany looked like. Love has little to do with the outsides of things.

Tiffany was in a cage across from mine. The space between didn't allow for us to touch noses, which was just as well. I'd have made a real fool of myself, I know I would.

She welcomed me with a wag of her slim, pointed tail. She was so tall that the top of her head touched the ceiling of her cage. She asked where I'd come from.

Well, I should have said the pound and let it go at that, but her eyes invited all kinds of things from me, so I found myself telling her my whole life story.

"You're a working dog," she said. She admired that, you could tell.

"I've got to find the sheep," I explained. "Old Dex is getting ready to retire, and Dad's going to need me."

Her eyes said something I didn't understand then. It was as if she could see things I couldn't, knew things I didn't.

"You'll find your sheep," she said.

I finally remembered my manners and asked where she'd come from.

"A great mansion," she said, "but that was long ago."

"A mansion?"

She described a magnificent house where she'd once lived so vividly that I can see it in my mind to this day. What impressed me most was her pillow. It was covered with dark blue velvet, she said, and had diamonds sewn into it. She didn't care for the diamonds—velvet, diamonds, I had to ask her to stop and explain everything. She said they dug into her delicate skin.

"What a great life!" I said.

"Yes," she said, but she didn't sound like she meant it. "A pillowed life. But when my sweet master died, the mistress sold me to the circus. Life has been quite different since."

"But why are you caged? Why is everybody in a cage?"

She didn't answer that. Thinking back, I realize it was kind of her not to. No use learning the worst until you had to.

"Everybody will tell you the same thing," she said. "Just do what Billy says. It isn't a good life, I won't lie to you. But he feeds us, gives us a home, such as it is." She looked around her small cage, especially small for her. "It could be worse. We could be out on the streets."

"It's not so bad out on the streets," I said.

I could tell she didn't believe me.

We weren't the only ones having a conversation. All around us were languages I'd never heard before, elephant and horse talk, monkey chatter. It was thrilling in its way, so much to learn. But I hated that cage. I decided right then not only to do what Billy wanted but to do it better than he expected. I'd use every bit of my brain and my athletic skill. I'd show him I wasn't meant to be caged. I'd work as hard for him as I'd have worked for Bob, as long as he let me be free.

You're way ahead of me, aren't you?

❂

I didn't work the next day. I didn't even know what kind of work I was going to do, some sort of herding I figured. The monkeys maybe. They couldn't even make a decent line.

Instead, I got to watch the show. At the end of my chain, sad to say, but was it ever exciting!

The horses came out first, all four of them. They ran around in a ring with pink ladies on their backs doing handstands and flips. The kids cheered like anything, so did their parents. There weren't a whole lot of people, but they made up for that with a lot of noise.

Next came the elephants. Boy, were they something, with their big, rolling, dark eyes. Kind of sad, though. You could see they didn't like their job, which was mostly to walk around with things on their backs, holding each other's tails. The smallest one, a female, had to sit down on a big, round stool. Then she had to dance on her back feet. If she didn't, she got yelled at and poked with a stick.

The biggest one, an old male, kept leaving dung piles behind him, like he'd been saving it up for days. And the look he gave that trainer! It made a sheep eye seem like a puny thing.

Ooooooooooh! breathed the crowd. Above our heads a man in silvery skins was flying through the air. Just when he was about to fall, that exact second, another man in skins, who was hanging from a bar by his knees, grabbed his hands, and they went sailing off together. It was enough to take your breath away.

The dogs were great, too. Well, I have to say that. Dogs don't belong in the circus. They look ridiculous wearing clown collars and hats. Even Tiffany, whose job it was to pull a wagon with You and You Too in the back, looked silly in her pink tutu. Most of the dogs were your smaller breeds, terriers, spaniels, Chihuahuas. Billy had them all going at once, through hoops and tunnels, up ramps, around in circles. You and You Too balanced on rolling balls. Tiffany danced like that elephant, on her back paws. She was very graceful, but I had to look away. She'd lived in a mansion once. She'd slept on diamonds. How could she let him make her look so foolish?

Why did any of them?

The next day, I found out.

"Come on, Sparky," said Billy. The door to my cage screeched open. I guessed that it was morning. There was no way to tell in that barn, except that you woke up hungry.

Sparky? Did he mean me?

"Do it!" You Too yipped. "Just do what he says."

"I will," I said. "Don't worry." It was my chance to show Billy how smart I was, and I was ready.

The chain got attached to my collar, and I didn't fight it. "Heel!" he said, and I did.

I trotted beside him past the trailers where the workers lived. I waited while he opened the door to an old shed. He closed the door behind us.

There was nothing in that room, nothing to chase or herd. Dirt floor. A single window, high above. Through dirty glass, the gray sky lent whatever light there was.

But there were other things in there I didn't see at first. One was hanging on the wall. Billy went over and took it down. It was made of leather and looked like a snake. Later, I knew it for what it was: a whip. The other was a long, thin stick.

"Okay, let's see what you can do," Billy said. He coughed and spit a green gob into the corner. Then he turned back to me.

Billy was the worst smelling human I've ever encountered. Worse than Hollerin, worse than elephant dung, worse than fish guts, worse than . . .

Well, you get my meaning. But one smell stood out above the others: meanness.

He started by whipping my back feet with that little stick. I jumped sideways. "Not that way," he hissed. "Flip!"

Flip? I tried my best to do what he said, I really did. But flip? What was flip?

He snapped my heels again. I jumped again, straight up this time.

That was when he started calling me names, ugly names, unrepeatable in polite company. He spit them out between his yellow, rotting teeth.

He was fat and couldn't move fast, but what he couldn't do that whip did. Down it came across my back. I yelped and ran to the door, leapt against it. It was a lot more solid than it looked.

He came at me with that whip, and I began to run, around and around that shed, dodging Billy at every turn.

He was patient, I'll give him that. He waited, stick in one hand, whip in the other, watching me run, an evil grin spread across his wet, red lips. Soon I was covered with sweat and panting hard. Fear gave me strength, but even fear wears you out over time. I could see he wasn't going to give up.

I had to stop. I had to figure out what flip was.

It took longer than it should have, smart as I am. But I wasn't made to do flips. What good is a flip to a flock of sheep? A couple more flicks with that stick against my heels and I went over backward. Surprised myself.

"Again!" said Billy, flicking the stick, and over I went.

But after all of it, after I'd learned flip, and roll (the easiest one), and stalk—basically what Old Dex did with the sheep, it was back on the chain and then back in the cage.

You, You Too, Tiffany, and the rest of the dogs were waiting. "How was it?" asked You. The dogs were anxious, concerned. I was among friends.

I told them about flip, how hard it was at first. But they knew all about it. "Sparky did those," You Too said. "Until . . . well."

Nobody said anything then.

"What?" I said. "Until what?"

The dogs all looked at each other. "Until he bit Billy," Tiffany said.

"He did?"

"Got him a good one on the hand," said You.

"What happened then?" I had to ask, even though I knew it would be bad. I could see it in Tiffany's eyes.

"Billy beat him," said You.

"To death," said You Too.

"It was terrible," said Tiffany, with a shudder. "Terrible."

9

YOU'RE PROBABLY WONDERING by now why I didn't take off. All that big talk about being free. I wondered about that myself sometimes. I had my chances. Instead of doing flips during our show, I could have run for the exit. I wasn't chained then. The tent didn't have real doors.

The Goat Man wouldn't have stayed for a minute.

At first, I thought it was Tiffany. It was, I guess. Freedom in exchange for love, not a bad trade. We were never left alone, but we had wonderful talks, long into the night, or lay with our noses as close as we could get them, which was never close enough. During the show, while the terriers ran through their flaming hoops, I'd brush against her long legs. She'd lean down and touch my nose. It was, well, there's no use explaining the nose thing. You'd never get it.

I still dreamed about the sheep, still felt something pulling me toward my destiny. But then I'd look into Tiffany's gleaming brown eyes and I'd forget the sheep. For a little while anyway.

Time went by. I did what Billy wanted. Tried not to remember that it was beneath me. I cringed to think what Dad would think, watching me flip over and over, over and over. I knew what Old Dex would have said about my clown collar.

I just kept telling myself that it was easier than life on the outside. And in its way, it was. As long as you didn't fight Billy.

Then it happened, as all things happen. Billy went too far.

He was smarter than he looked. He'd seen the way Tiffany and I looked at each other. He came for us one morning, and we followed him to the shed. I tried to look brave, to hide my shaking.

He opened the door and closed it behind us. I began to feel sick. What would he want me to do this time? What if I didn't understand? I didn't want to look foolish, not with Tiffany watching. I'd told her about Old Dex and Dad, how smart and brave they were, all the time hoping she'd think the same about me.

Billy lifted his stick. "Dance!" he said, and up Tiffany went on her long legs, front paws draped in front of her.

It was hard for me to watch. At last he let her stop.

"Okay, now you," he said to me. "Dance!"

It would have been easy enough, balancing on my hind legs, turning in circles. But I couldn't.

"You heard me, Sparky!" Billy yelled. "Dance!"

I held my ground.

"What are you, some kind of moron? I said *dance*!"

Tiffany nudged my ear. "Do it," she whispered. "You have to!"

I tried to tell her with my eyes what I couldn't say in words.

Billy went for the whip. "Dance!" he yelled. His whip cracked the air.

And I held my ground.

"What's the matter?" asked Tiffany, a worried look in her eyes.

I couldn't explain, not without hurting her feelings. How could I tell her how foolish she looked? How could I explain what a dog's life was meant to be? Dancing is downright humiliating for a dog. It goes against nature. There's a line you just can't cross and still be who you are. Billy was asking me to cross that line.

Down came that whip. I didn't yelp this time. Not with Tiffany watching, my pain reflected in her eyes.

"Dance, you mangy cur!"

Snap went the whip.

Still I held my ground.

For a little while, and strangely, my life began to re-live itself. I heard Dad's voice, felt Mom's lick, saw Bob riding Appie. I remembered the Goat Man's laugh, and how it felt to run with the sheep.

Down came the whip again and again. Tiffany never

looked away. My eyes never left hers. Not until the blackness took over.

✹

"Are you awake?"

Was this what it meant to die? I couldn't lift a paw, could hardly breathe. It hurt too much even to whimper. My back and sides stung like the memory of fire. Pain had settled deep within me, a dark and angry presence. Something trickled from my side, I didn't want to think what.

Tiffany began to lick my face, long, soft licks to soothe me. I closed my eyes. How had she gotten into my cage? Was I dreaming? If so, it was better to dream than to be awake. I drifted off again.

Several times during the night I awoke, but feeling her beside me, I could let myself go back to that dark and dreamless world where time stood still.

Morning brought no relief, except that Tiffany was there.

"I have to go," she said. "Lie still. Rest." She licked my eyelids.

Food arrived, but I had gone to that place beyond hunger, beyond caring. I think for a time I was close to death.

One of the workers came and dressed my wounds. She was kind and tried to soothe me with words. After she left, I was alone. The others had gone to perform.

73

The cheering sounded distant, as if it were moving farther and farther away from me.

It was many days before I could stand, before I could eat the food they brought. Each night Tiffany would stay by my side—she'd always been able to open the cages, I couldn't understand why she hadn't left that place long before.

❊

I slept and dreamed, but never about the sheep. I knew it was because I'd lost my purpose. I'd given in to a caged life. Hour after hour, I lay on the cold dirt floor feeling sorry for myself. Every time the door opened, I cringed, knowing it had to be Billy. But it never was. He wasn't sorry about what he'd done to me, that wasn't why he stayed away. He simply had no use for me now that I couldn't perform. But he hadn't forgotten me. He wasn't the kind to give up, to let the dancing trick go; he was waiting, that's all, waiting for me to get well enough to work again. Either that, or die. He didn't care which.

At long last, I recovered. I began to eat with a good appetite. I looked forward to seeing my friends return from the day's performance. They never said what I knew was in their minds: Billy would come for me, and soon.

❊

It was on a cold morning. We'd been fed and were waiting to be taken to the tent. Sometimes one of the trainers would come for us. This time it was Billy. To smell the man again made me sick inside. When he opened my cage, I couldn't make my legs move. But the little dogs urged me in their worried voices, "Do what he says! You've got to!"

"Get out here," Billy said, his voice like a crack of that whip.

I did what he said.

We crossed the frozen ground to the tent, Tiffany at my side, the little dogs all around. There wasn't much anybody could do if Billy decided to hurt me again, but I knew they'd be there for me if they could. Especially Tiffany. She was brave in that way—for others, never for herself.

The elephants were restless, especially the big one they called Karma. Elephants don't like the cold, as a rule. As we dogs passed on our way into the ring, Karma threw back his big trunk and trumpeted. The audience gasped, and then they began to applaud. Karma's trainer poked and poked at him, trying to make him bow on one knee, his trick at the end of the elephant show. But Karma just bellowed, dancing away from the stick.

This is what I've come to know about elephants: they are not slow. They might look slow, but they're one heck of a lot faster than sheep, and a whole lot more dangerous.

Billy was restless, too, cursing under his breath, just loud enough for us to hear. With his big checkered clown suit and painted-on smile, he looked as if he was having a great time. But every now and then he'd stop and stare at me as if I'd beat him at some game.

"Ready for a dancing lesson, Sparky?" he said, his yellow teeth grinning inside that shiny, red mouth. Then he laughed his awful, broken laugh. "After the show, boy. You'll dance for me then, won't you?"

All the time he was talking to me and my heart was shrinking inside, Billy was buckling on the harness. My job for the day was to pull You and You Too in the cart, while Tiffany danced. Around and around we went, past the elephants, past the cheering children. It was a mule's job. Not that I was better than a mule, mind you. I'd had bigger dreams once, that's all.

At Billy's order we came to a stop. Then he grabbed a hoop and set it on fire. A cloud of stinking black smoke rose up inside the tent. I hated this part. The whole time the little dogs did their fire trick, I'd want to run away, race ahead of the sheep and Bob and back to my mom.

Then I'd remember where I was and try to be strong for the others.

"Jump, dogs!" Billy commanded, and all the little dogs lined up. One by one they ran and jumped through the burning hoop, then back around the ring and through the hoop again. They were so brave. But I guess, after all, they were more afraid of Billy than they were of fire.

The audience loved that trick. They gasped and cheered as the dogs leapt clear of the flames and around the ring. Everything was going as it always had when, suddenly, the tip of You's hat caught fire. Away he ran, the fire blazing behind him.

"You!" cried You Too. Or maybe it was all of us. When You realized his hat was on fire, he went a little crazy. Up he scrambled onto the back of a horse. The pink lady rider screamed as her costume caught fire. She slid off the horse and began rolling on the ground. You kept running, setting everything his hat touched on fire. Flags and banners, ropes and feathers, my wooden cart. Then everything happened at once. People screamed and began to push and run. The horses went one way, the elephants another. Karma went straight for the crowd.

I moved without thinking. My flaming cart bouncing behind me, I headed straight for Karma. It was no time for manners. I went for his back foot and sank my teeth in. Or tried to. If you've ever tried to bite into elephant hide, you know how tough it is. Karma hardly knew I was there. He raced for the door, where the people were crowded trying to get out, his big eye rolling. With a burst of speed, I got ahead of him and leapt for his throat. This slowed him down a little. At least he knew I was there. He did a little hop sideways, graceful as any animal I've ever seen. I leapt again, nipping his bottom lip. Up came his front feet. Back went his big trunk, and he bellowed like he was dying.

I danced away from those huge feet as they came down, right onto my flaming cart, and broke it in pieces. I shook free of the cart, but the harness came with me. The last of the people pushed through the door as Karma's trainer came running, his costume torn and covered with soot. While I'd been herding his elephant for him, he must have been helping the pink lady.

The ring was filled with swirls of color, costumes, painted faces, clown collars, smoke, snorting horses, bellowing elephants, barking dogs as the trainers tried to calm their animals and Billy ran everywhere yelling.

It didn't take a genius to figure it out. It was our chance to escape.

I found Tiffany trying to calm a terrier with a singed paw.

"Let's go!" I said. "It's our chance! Let's get out of here!"

She looked at me with the saddest expression. She didn't say, "What chance?" She didn't say, "Go where?"

"Come on!" I said.

You and You Too were leading the little dogs out the door like it was any other day, going back to their cages without even being told. They had never known the sweet taste of freedom, and now they never would.

Flames raced up one side of the tent, leaving a gaping hole through which I could see the sky.

Tiffany licked the injured terrier's paw. She nudged him to his feet. Fire was reaching for the top of the tent. From a long way off, sirens screamed.

I butted Tiffany with my nose. "Come *on*!" I said.

Tiffany turned to me, gazed down into my eyes. It seemed forever until she said, "Go. You have to go."

"But you have to come with me!"

"I can't," she said. "Don't you see? I can't. I have to stay."

If you'd seen her eyes, you'd have known nothing I could say or do would make her change her mind.

"Run for both of us," she said. "Find your sheep."

I touched her nose for the last time with mine. "I will," I said. "I promise."

Then I headed fast as my legs could run toward that blue, blue sky.

10

I RAN as straight and fast as the world would allow, putting as many miles between me and Billy as I could. I crossed roads, skirted houses and people and cars. With never a thought of hunger or weariness, I ran for my life. If I began to flag, Tiffany's words urged me on, giving me the strength of two. Run for both of us, she'd said.

I had no idea where I was until the country began to look familiar. When I came to the field of weeds, I slowed down. It was only then that I realized how dreadfully thirsty I was, and how tired. I made my way across the field the way I'd followed Snatch and Hollerin, stopping to drink from a puddle. How great it would be, I thought, if they were back from California.

But what then? Did I really want to be a thief again? Was that all life had in store for me? Run for both of us wasn't all Tiffany had said. She'd told me to find the sheep, *my* sheep. While Billy had me under lock and key, I couldn't. While I was under Tiffany's spell, I wouldn't. Now I didn't know if I had it in me anymore.

Trotting along, deep in thought, I didn't notice the boy on the tracks because I was feeling so sorry for myself. I was starting to believe I'd never find the sheep, never regain my purpose in life. Hard as it is to own up to such shameful thoughts, I was about to give in. I was about to settle for being, well, a dog. Your everyday fetch-the-slippers-get-the-paper dog. It was painful to settle for less than I was worth, but I wasn't getting any younger. Life on the road can wear a soul to ribbons, that's the truth.

And then I heard the train whistle, loud and shrill. It woke me right up.

The boy was walking the tracks. Balancing himself with his arms out, playing dare-you-to-hit-me or something. Foolish thing to do with something hundreds of times your size. He wore dirty blue jeans, and his hair stuck out from his head like weeds, a mutt of a kid.

That whistle again, this time real impatient, and the boy jumped off. I was right behind him, got there so fast it surprised me. But I was ready. The boy looked down on the ground, stuck his hands in his pockets, searching for something. Then he saw it, whatever it was, on the tracks and made a dive for it. Thing is, so did I. I hit that boy from behind like he was a four-hundred-pound sheep. He went flying right off the bank, me tumbling behind, as the train rushed by, all cinders and metal and scream.

I got up and shook the dirt off, but the boy didn't.

He lay there on the hard-packed dirt so still, I figured I'd killed him, blood trickling from a cut on his chin. I licked his face all over—it needed a good washing—and at last his eyes opened. You could see he didn't know what hit him.

"Hi, dog," he said.

✦

The kid got up and brushed himself off. "Whoa!" he said. "What happened?" Away down the tracks went that train, no more than a black speck. He watched it disappear, still trying to figure out what had happened to him. And then I guess he did. "Whoa!" he said again, shaking his head. "You saved my life!"

Then his eyes got wider. "Oh, no!" he cried. "My stopwatch!" He ran back up to the tracks, knelt down, and started sifting through the stones and stuff. There wasn't much of that watch left to save, but he put a couple of the bigger pieces in his pocket. "It was my dad's," he said, his eyes getting puffy and red. "My dad was a famous runner."

Well, so was mine.

Still, I could tell it meant a lot to him that his dad was famous, and I felt bad about his watch. His dad would sure be mad if he knew what really happened, how the kid had almost lost his life over a dumb watch. At the same time, I was feeling pretty good about what I'd done. The old herding habits were still with me. I trotted on, leaving the kid behind. He'd have to face the music on his own; I was hungry.

"Hey! Dog! Wait up!" He hurried to catch me. Stuffing his hands into his pockets, he began walking alongside. You could tell he needed the company, and I really didn't mind.

"Who do you belong to anyway?" he said. He knelt down, and I let him check my harness for a tag. "Are you lost? I'll bet you're lost, huh, boy?" He roughed me up in a good way, scratching behind my ears, patting me hard all over. "You saved my life! You should get a reward!"

A nice hunk of meat was what I was thinking. But this kid didn't look like he had the money for a hot dog.

I followed him away from the tracks, toward the town. "I gotta hang out till school's over," the kid says, "or I'm in real trouble. Come on, I'll show you where you can get free food."

We took the back streets, a good idea for us both. We were on the lam, as they say. No way was I ever going to spend another night in a cage. But that meant keeping my eyes open not only for Billy but for the truck from the pound. The kid was being careful, too, too careful if you know what I mean. This kid has no home, was what I was thinking.

But I was wrong.

"That's where I live, over there." Like he'd read my mind. He pointed to a chain-link fence and a long, yellow brick building across a scruffy lawn. "It's the Good Shepherd Home for Boys," he said.

I stopped dead in my tracks. The kid lived with a shepherd! From where we were standing, I couldn't see the sheep. Grazing in a nearby field probably. I couldn't believe my good fortune.

"Come on, boy," the kid said. "They'll see me."

We crossed the street, went a couple of blocks, then scooted across a parking lot to the back of a pizza parlor. The kid looked all around, then began rooting through a trash can. I hung back. The smells inside that can—whew! "It's our lucky day!" he said, pulling out a pizza box. "Pepperoni. Wrong order, I'll bet."

You didn't think dogs liked pepperoni pizza, did you? The trouble is the salt. Makes a fella thirsty as all get out. But food is food. We finished off that pizza and headed away from the main street again. I marked some spots along the way, all the while looking for water. But it was a good many blocks before I saw a water fountain in a park. I ran right over, jumped up, and turned it on. Took a long, slow drink. Was that ever satisfying!

The kid couldn't believe his eyes. "Wow! Are you a trick dog or what? How did you do that?"

I hate being underestimated. Call it pride, but what's so hard about turning on a water fountain? That kid hadn't seen the half of it, and I wasn't about to show him either. I'd had my fill of tricks.

"You need a name," the kid said. It was that time after a meal when a fella needs a nap, but the kid was too old for a nap. Well, too old to think he needed one. After having run half the morning, I had only one thing in mind—a good snooze—but I trotted along beside him as if we'd been pals for years. When it came time to meet the Good Shepherd, I was going to be ready.

Well, you can guess what I was thinking, who I was thinking about. I could almost smell the coffee on him, taste his big, rough hand. Now, I knew the Good Shepherd couldn't be Bob. Still, it was hard not to mush things all up in my mind until, when we finally turned back the way we came, I almost believed I'd see Bob come strolling out of that yellow brick building, Old Dex and Dad at his side. Dad would come running over. We'd sniff each other nose to tail until we got our fill. "We missed you, son," Dad would say. Then Bob would . . .

Meanwhile, the kid was busy naming me. I'd gotten used to it. Blackie, Shep, Spot, and the worst one ever, Sparky. Names are for people's convenience, you know, so they can call us when they get lost. Dogs don't need names.

"I know!" the kid said after some real deep thought. "Jack!" Jack. Can't say I wasn't surprised. Jack. Not your usual dog name. I rolled it around my brain. Jack. It had a good ring to it. Nothing fancy. Salt of the earth kind of name. I gave the kid a woof of approval, and he caught right on. I figured him for one of those genius types, quick to pick things up. But he belonged in school. We'd passed a red brick one with a playground, some swings, a big field. He didn't act real interested, just stuck his head way down into the collar of his jacket and we moved right on.

✪

The Good Shepherd Home for Boys didn't invite you right in. The windows were small and pinched looking, like mean little eyes, and the front door scowled, telling you that whatever you did was wrong. The kid stopped with his hand on the big brass knob. "You gotta wait out here, Jack," he said. "Don't worry, I'll find you a place to sleep and some food."

This was okay with me. I was going to do some sniffing around anyway. The place didn't smell right, and it sure didn't smell like sheep. If the Good Shepherd kept his sheep somewhere else, I'd have to find them. That could take some time. The kid knelt down and hugged me, putting his whole heart into it. "Don't go away. Okay, Jack? We're buddies now, right?"

Just then the door opened, and a big, beefy kid came pushing out. "Hey, Retardo! You cut school again, didn'tcha? You're in trouble now!" He gave the kid a push on the shoulder, knocking him back.

The kid looked down at his feet, letting the bigger boy pass. Retardo was a nice kid, I felt bad for him.

Didn't he know you couldn't give in to a bully like that?

There I was starting to worry about a human when all I wanted was my freedom and some sheep. I waited until the kid went inside, then took off.

There wasn't much to see. Yellow bricks, chain-link fence all around the back. A playground, no swings. I sniffed everything, casing the joint as Snatch used to say. All the usual smells—dog, dust, bugs, weeds, rubber, a penny, gum, cigarette butts, sadness.

Two boys came out of the building. They leaned against the bricks with their hands in their pockets, looking down at their feet. No Retardo. It was dinnertime, or close to it, and I was getting mighty hungry. I kept thinking about an Italian restaurant that had the best sausage and a cook who liked dogs. But Retardo, what was I going to do about him? What if he was getting whipped? And here I was dreaming about sausage!

Well, he wasn't my responsibility. Like the Goat Man used to say, you have to take care of yourself first. Then you can lend a hand to others. But he never said anything about lending a paw.

Funny how life is. If the Goat Man had stuck around, my life would have been a whole lot easier. I'd have learned everything there is to know. As it turned out, I learned the hard way, which isn't always so bad, the hard way being a whole lot better than learning nothing at all.

11

AFTER I LEFT RETARDO, the night was pretty much a bust all around. No sausage and no sheep anywhere. My paws were tired and my spirits low by the time I turned back toward the Good Shepherd. The kid had promised food and a place to bed down. I'd see if he was as good as his word.

He was waiting by the door, slumped over with his forehead on his knees and his arms wrapped around them. I guess it was later than I thought. I licked his hand, and he woke right up. "Jack!" He threw his arms around me. "Jack boy! Good dog! I knew you'd come back." And all that sort of thing, pounding me half to death.

"Okay, so here's the plan," he said. "I got to sneak you in. No way will they let a dog in there. So we gotta be real quiet, okay?"

What I liked about Retardo right off was that he talked to me man to man, or person to dog I should say. He knew me for the smart dog I am. I began to belong with him because of that, because he knew my worth.

Retardo reached for the door handle. "Okay, let's go," he said. The door shushed open. Fingers of cold air came reaching out. My nose sniffed for information. Floor wax, soapsuds, boiled cabbage, sorrow. I followed Retardo, who scurried ahead in a low crouch. I guess he thought he'd be smaller that way, invisible. But the crouch is basically an attack position, any half-grown sheep knows that. This kid had a lot to learn.

The hall was dark and quiet. I could hear the soft breathing of children asleep nearby, a peaceful sound. But a clock ticked overhead as if we were stealing its minutes, no-no no-no no-no no-no. Paper rustled in a room as we passed. Then I heard footsteps.

"Quick! In here!" Retardo closed the door quickly behind us. The room was long and narrow with high windows. Squares of moonlight fell upon the beds, each with a lump in it the size of a boy (well, a child, but they were all boys as it turned out).

"Under here," Retardo said, lifting a corner of the thin blanket on a narrow bed. "I'll find you some food. But you have to wait here and be real quiet." He reached under the blanket and pulled out a bunch of musty towels he'd stuffed there to look like he'd been sleeping all along. Those went under the bed with me. Then I was alone.

There was not one speck of dust under that bed, not a bug or a cobweb. Made me uneasy. It seemed unnatural. Dirt was a necessary part of the things kids did, like playing softball and building forts. They liked dirt. What kind of a place was this?

I waited, listening.

Footsteps. I held real still, in case it wasn't the kid.

"I'm sorry, Jack," Retardo said, reaching under the bed to pat me with an empty hand. I liked the smell of his hand, boy sweat, a good, honest smell. "They lock everything up in there. I'll bet you're real hungry, aren't you, boy? I'll make it up to you. I promise. I'll think of something." His eyes were so sad.

He lay beside me for a while on the floor, his hand on my back. After a while, he said good night and climbed into bed. I fell into a half sleep, the watchful kind.

It wasn't long before the door opened and a shaft of light sliced the room in two. I woke right up, banging my head on the bedsprings. I heard a boy stir in a nearby bed; another called out of a dream. A loud sniff came from the direction of the door. Whoever it was had a good nose for a human.

Laced-up boots marched down the space that separated the two rows of beds. They came to a stop at Retardo's, within inches of my nose. Shiny black boots, long black stockings. Up came a corner of the blanket.

Eyes like raisins poked in dough stared hard at me. Down went the blanket.

The bed began shaking back and forth. "Luke! Wake up. Luke! There's a dog under your bed."

Well, I knew she meant Retardo. I just didn't know Retardo was his bad name, the one the other kids called him because he couldn't read.

"Get up! Get out of that bed!"

Luke yawned and whined as if he'd been asleep, but I'd felt him awaken the second the door opened. "What dog?" he said, in that innocent voice boys find when they need it.

A hand reached down and threw the covers clean off the bed. "*That* dog!" said the lady. Then Luke's face appeared upside down. At the back of his neck was the dough lady's knotty hand. Luke grinned. "Hi, Jack," he said.

By then the whole place was awake. Boys in striped pajamas swarmed around Luke's bed like sheep. "There's a dog! Retardo's got a dog!"

"Back!" screeched the lady. "Back in your beds, every last one of you!"

A couple of the smaller boys melted away, but the others had fixed their eyes on me as I stood at Luke's side. He wasn't good for a meal or, as it turned out, for a bed either, but he'd done his best. Whatever would befall us, would befall us together.

There was hunger in the eyes of those sleepy boys, and not the kind that food settles. You could see they needed to hug a dog, every last one of them. But the woman was having none of that. She stuck a whistle into her doughy face and began blowing and blowing. I wanted to bury my head in my paws. It was shriller than the train whistle.

Other grownups came then. The boys were herded back to their beds.

"You!" The woman pointed her finger straight at Luke's nose. "Come with me."

She turned to a young man with a bunch of keys weighing him down. "Get that . . . that mutt out of here!"

Talk about your low blows!

"Jack!" cried Luke, but the lady had him by the ear and was dragging him out the door.

I gave him a little woof for courage and headed for the door myself. I knew which way was out, always have.

The man with the keys was all right. He talked to me in the hall the way people do. You know, nonsense stuff. "Good dog, that's the way, come along, that's it, like a good dog now, here we go." He patted me on the head a couple of times and opened the door.

Goodbye, Good Shepherd.

It was a full moon night, a night you want to be nestled on a hillside, the sheep hunkered down, dreaming whatever sheep dream. I was regretting not having given that dough lady's hand a good nip. Not an all-out bite. I could tell by her wrinkled-up face that she wasn't a mean soul. She had a job to do and was doing her best to see that it got done. I could understand that. The problem is that children aren't sheep.

Somewhere along the way that woman lost sight of what a real boy is, mostly what a real boy needs. Food, sure. A warm bed to snuggle into at the end of a long day. But a boy needs love most of all. A boy needs to be told he's a good dog.

Good boy, I mean.

Well, there isn't as much difference as you'd think. Treat a dog like he's worthless and that's the way he'll turn out. Same thing for boys. I could tell by the way Luke carried himself, his shoulders already hunched, that he had no idea of his worth, what he could do in the world if he was given half a chance. Too many years like that and he'd be acting as mean as Billy.

Deep in my canine soul, I knew one sure thing: Luke had to get away from that place. The Good Shepherd had nothing to do with it as far as I could tell.

12

THERE WASN'T MUCH I could do for Luke once the dough lady sent me packing. I headed away from the home with no plan for what to do next. Something about this kid had me stuck in that no-sheep town, always watching my back for Billy or the truck from the pound. The kid needed me. I guess that was it. He needed me like nobody else ever had.

Sniffing my way down the street, I kept thinking about all those boys. I couldn't figure out what they were doing in that place. Had they all run away from home? Were they captured one at a time like stray dogs? Why didn't their moms and dads come and get them back?

From my short time at the pound, I remembered the happy reunions between dogs and their owners. But some dogs got stuck there too long. There were terrible stories about what happened to you if you didn't get a home, stories that made my fur stand on end.

They wouldn't do that to boys, though, would they?

By instinct I had been moving toward the darker

end of town, onto streets with broken streetlights and boarded-up houses. People in the darker places were easier on dogs. As a rule, they didn't get all worked up over a tipped trash can. You got your higher-quality garbage in the better neighborhoods, but you could end up paying for it with your freedom.

I turned into the yard of a house with a wide, sagging porch and nice thick bushes to hide in. To look at the place, you'd have thought nobody had ever lived there, but the porch underneath was a regular rat hotel. I stuck my nose in, and the tenants ran in all directions. Which was fine with me. Sleeping with rats isn't my idea of a good night's rest. They never settle down. Always scratching or sniffing. I don't know how they get any sleep at all.

But I wasn't sleeping so well myself. Too much on my mind. Billy, Tiffany, You and You Too. Had it been right for me to run? Shouldn't I have stayed, stuck it out with my friends? Tried harder to talk them into leaving?

What did my life amount to anyway? Was it even worth saving? The truth, it seemed to me then, was that I wasn't getting anywhere. I'd come no closer to where I belonged. In all my time on the road, I'd seen exactly two sheep. *Two!* And they were stuck in a truck. All I got there was a snoot full of memory.

Where was my life going now that I was free again? Without honest work, what good was I? I was a beggar and a thief, nothing more. I knew the Goat Man wouldn't be proud of me, and I didn't even want to think about Dad. A smarter dog would have found the sheep by now. It was another fitful night, just me and my thoughts and those rats.

Morning came at last. Light seeped in under the porch. My hiding place was dismal in the morning light—broken bottles, cigarette butts, a bicycle wheel threaded with spiderwebs. I crawled out, did a couple of rolls in the dust to get the kinks out. I wasn't in a very good mood, and my empty stomach ached. I started back toward the home, giving my ugliest sheep eye to every cat that crossed my path. Scared the heck out of a lady's Chihuahua, too, but then everything scares those skinny little things.

Something new! A long white banner was stretched across the chain-link fence at the Good Shepherd Home for Boys. There were words on it and stick figure drawings of people walking into the Home and coming out with boys.

So that was it! The Good Shepherd Home was a pound for boys. They lived there until their parents came back, or somebody else adopted them. Adoption was all the dogs ever talked about at the pound. Man, did they ever carry on when the people came. All but me and the sheepdog. We learned to let our best selves shine. Then Billy came and, well, you know the rest.

Luke was waiting at the end of the fence. As soon as

he saw me, a big grin broke out on his face and he came running, waving something in the air.

"Hey, Jack! Guess what I got for you! A bone!"

Well, it was a bone all right, not a shred of meat on the thing. But I gnawed on it some to make the kid happy. I could only guess what he'd gone through to find me the very thing he thought a dog would love.

Somebody had cleaned Luke up. He was wearing his Sunday-go-to-meeting clothes—that's what the Goat Man called them—and his haystack hair was slicked down with something sweet-smelling and sticky.

"Come on," he said. "There's a place where you can hang out and wait for me. It's Adoption Week. I gotta do this dumb lineup thing again." He waved for me to follow. "Hey, don't forget your bone!"

I followed him around the side of the building. When we got to a narrow doorway, he stopped and looked around to see if anybody was watching. "There's just tools and stuff in here. I found a rug for you to sleep on." He opened the door to a small room, dark and musty, smelling of gasoline. It was jammed with tools, like the kid said, and the usual cobwebs. Never stop spinning, those spiders. On the floor was a nice little striped rug.

But I couldn't go inside, not even for Luke.

"Come on, boy," he said, stepping in. "It's all right."

But it wasn't.

"What's the matter, Jack?" He knelt down and began to pet me. I could tell that he was trying real hard to understand. But even with people language, how could I have explained what it's like to be locked up? Even the home didn't lock the boys inside. I knew Luke wouldn't do that to me, but somebody else might. I couldn't take the chance. Luke unbuckled my harness and gave me a rubdown.

"Luke! Lucassssss!!"

Luke jumped up. "Criminy! That's Mrs. Pinch! I gotta go." He bolted out of the toolroom, dragging my harness behind him. "Wait for me, Jack!" I heard him call. "I won't be long. Nobody ever picks me."

That stopped me in my tracks. What did he mean nobody ever picked him? What kind of people wouldn't pick Luke? I had to see these people who came to Adoption Week. If they didn't like Luke, they couldn't be very smart.

I hung around until several cars and one old pickup truck pulled into the parking lot. As the people got out, I looked them over. They seemed okay to me. For people, I mean. A little serious, but that was to be expected. You didn't want to adopt a dog or a kid if you hadn't thought a whole lot about it. I mean, it isn't like getting a fish or a rabbit.

Then I saw the perfect folks for Luke. They got out of the pickup and crossed the parking lot, hand in hand. The lady had a round, pink face, a happy kind of face. The man made me think of Bob. He was shorter and younger than Bob, but he walked with that same sure stride. And his hair? It was like Luke's without the sticky stuff, a real haystack.

My stomach was growling something fierce, but I had to see what would happen. I had to see the look on Luke's face when his new folks picked him.

The windows on this side of the building were long and low to the ground. That made it easy for me to look in. Most of the rooms were empty. Well, empty of people. There was furniture and stuff. Then I found the room with the kids. I crouched low so that I couldn't be seen, stuck my nose on the ledge, and watched.

The boys were all dressed like Luke, with dark pants and clean white shirts. They stood in a single line, their hands at their sides. They weren't like the dogs at the pound. You could see they were trying very hard to behave. The tall ones stood with their shoulders back, like soldiers. The smallest ones looked a little frightened.

I didn't see Luke at first, and then I did. He was at the very end of the line, scowling down at his shined-up shoes. His fists were stuffed into his pockets.

On the other side of the room stood the parents. I mean, the people who wanted to be parents. They looked a little frightened, too. The dough lady Luke called Mrs. Pinch was there, and so was a tall man with gray patches of hair on his head and a very long nose. I couldn't hear what the man was saying, but his mouth kept moving for a very long time. I saw the boys laughing at something he said.

All the boys but Luke. Luke never looked up, not once, and he didn't laugh at all.

Then there was all this shaking of hands. Strangest thing. In their long line, the boys walked up, did this little bow, and shook each person's hand. The parent people smiled and looked the boys over as they passed like, well, like sheep.

Luke was the last in line. He slumped along with hunched shoulders, dragging his feet. He shook hands without looking up once, not even when he got to the perfect folks.

It was downright discouraging. What was the matter with the kid? Did he like living with the dough lady? Didn't he want a real home? I watched until several of the boys had been picked and left holding the hands of their proud new parents. The folks with the pickup left without anybody.

When Luke came out, I couldn't even look at him.

"Come on," he said, as if he were mad at me. But I knew he wasn't. "Let's get out of here.

"I don't care about any of that stuff," he said, kicking a stone halfway across the parking lot. "Bunch of dumb people. I wish old Pinch and them wouldn't make us do that. They just want to get rid of us, is all.

Especially us big kids. Nobody ever picks us, no matter what we do!"

But you don't even try, I wanted to say. Even the boy who'd pushed Luke around had been trying his best to get some parents. He stood straight and tall, like he was proud of himself. He shook hands like he really meant it. Not Luke.

Well, that boy didn't get chosen either. But he'd tried. You had to respect that.

We left the home behind, Luke scuffing his feet as if they were too heavy to pick up. He was wearing his old clothes again and his torn tennis shoes. "There's probably something the matter with me," he muttered. "I mean, besides the reading. Things get mixed up in my head sometimes. It's probably in the records. Probably says I'm crazy or something."

We crossed several streets. Luke kept wiping his runny nose on his sleeve. "At least I got the quarter. We all get one for being good. Hey, I know! Let's get an ice cream."

You know how ice cream can cheer a soul right up, but I'd never tasted any till that day. Luke bought us a vanilla ice cream cone, and we shared it sitting on the sidewalk. People kept stopping and smiling at us, as if we were putting on a show. If Billy had been there, he'd have charged admission.

But I didn't want to think about Billy, not ever again.

"My dad bought me an ice cream cone once," Luke said, taking a big swipe with his tongue. "That's why I always get vanilla. 'Cause it's what he bought me."

We were making a real mess of that ice cream, but it was real good. Not as good as goat's milk, but close.

Luke frowned. "My dad wasn't a famous runner, Jack. I just said that because . . . well, because that's what I tell everybody. The only time I ever saw my dad run was when the cops were chasing him. That was the *last* time I saw him, too."

He gave me the tip end of the cone. Then he wiped his mouth on his sleeve. "I never did have a mama, is the thing. Well, I guess I did when I was born, but I don't know what happened to her."

Luke turned out to be a real talker. Moms passed us pushing baby carriages. A little boy floated a balloon from his perch on his dad's shoulders. Luke kept right on talking. I think he'd been waiting a long time to stick all his words together. Now that he had somebody to listen, he wasn't about to quit.

"When my aunt called the home? I looked around for something of my dad's to keep, you know? Something to take with me. That's when I found the stopwatch." He reached into his pocket and took out the pieces he'd picked up off the tracks. He rubbed his thumb back and forth across the biggest piece.

I laid my head on Luke's lap, wagged my tail to let

him know I understood. He smiled then. It was like the sunrise, that smile. Like the sun forgetting the night it had left behind. There was still a lot of hope left in this kid. He had to have some folks, that's all. He *had* to.

I'd done my share of looking, and I knew.

13

IT WAS THE SECOND DAY of Adoption Week, and Luke hadn't learned a thing. I watched him from my post beneath the window ledge, hoping he'd catch on. He didn't. He just wore this long, ugly face and slumped along. Nobody wants a sulky dog. Boy, that is. And nobody was picking Luke. I found myself rooting for the guy who'd bullied Luke. At least he was trying. But nobody picked him this time either. I guessed Luke was right, people only wanted the little kids.

Well, they *were* cute. Like puppies, you know, only with people faces on them.

Luke came out after a while, in that same bad mood and with no money for ice cream this time.

His bad moods never lasted, though. That was another good thing about him.

"Let's go visit Raggedy Annie. She'll give us cookies and stuff. She gave me a dime once. All I did was sweep her porch."

The whole way there, Luke never stopped talking.

"Know how many times I didn't get picked?" He almost sounded proud, but I knew he wasn't. "Guess!"

Well, I just didn't want to, you know. It was going to be a sorry number, I was sure of that.

"Twenty-six times. First couple of times, I got real excited. I mean, it was like this big thing! Like you were going to win a prize if you were good. I *knew* I was going to be picked. I even dreamed it once, how I got these real cool folks and my own room all to myself."

Twenty-six times? That sounded like a lot. Was Adoption Week every week?

"I ran away once. I didn't want to stand in that line again, not even for a quarter."

Maybe the boys who smiled got two quarters. Did he ever think of that?

"The whole thing stinks," he said.

The give-up words. I'd heard them before from a couple of terriers.

He was still talking when we got to Raggedy Annie's. Some place that was. You never saw so much stuff. Bundles of rags were piled up all around her tiny house, in the yard, on the porch, on top of an old car. I just shook my head. You know, the way dogs do. People get the craziest ideas.

Raggedy Annie came to the door after Luke rang the big brass bell that was hanging beside it. "Well, look who's here!" she said, pushing back the screen. She had a friendly smile with only a few chewing teeth. "And you've brought a friend." That lady could hardly get through her door, that's how big she was. I could see then where she got her name, or where Luke got it. Because that's what she wore. Rags. They were tied around her head and around her big middle. Her faded dress was shredded along the bottom. Even her shoes were tied on with rags.

She leaned over and patted my head. "Nice doggie," she said. "I'll bet you'd like something to eat. Boys and dogs are always hungry."

Now here was one smart lady.

She went back inside, which took some doing.

"See? What did I tell you?" Luke whispered. "Rags and junk all over the place! I think she's a little, you know . . ." He twirled his finger around his ear. "But she's real nice."

He was right about the nice part. Out she came carrying a plate of cookies for Luke and a big, fat hot dog for me.

We chowed down while Raggedy Annie told us about her day. She'd been bundling all morning, she said, and now she was waiting for the truck to come. The rags weren't rags at all. They were old clothes. "Perfectly good clothes," she said. She collected them from all over. Nobody was as good at finding clothes as she was. You could tell she was proud of that.

Then, when there were so many piles she could hardly breathe, a truck would come and take them away. The clothes went to people who couldn't afford to buy any, is the way I understood it.

"Poor people?" asked Luke.

"Oh, yes," Raggedy Annie said. "So poor you can't even imagine. And you should see some of the clothes that get thrown away! *Well!*" she said. "Look at this!" She reached into a pile and pulled out a black, slinky thing with shiny stones on the sleeves. "And this!" Out came a coat made from the skins of rabbits. Never could understand why people dress themselves like animals. "Some of this looks brand-new!" She clicked her tongue. "Such waste."

Luke turned those cookies into crumbs in no time. Raggedy Annie took his plate, then narrowed her eyes at him. "You didn't bring your reading book, *did* you?"

Luke hung his head. "I forgot."

She sighed through her nose. "How are we ever going to get you up to speed if you don't practice?"

"I don't like reading," Luke said. He was whining again. Hurts a dog's ears, that sound. The kid gave up too easily. Raggedy Annie didn't like that any more than I did.

Her eyes went wide. "What kind of smart boy doesn't like to read?"

"I'm not smart," he said, scowling.

Raggedy Annie stuck her hands on her hips. "Well,

now I've heard it all. A smart boy who doesn't think he's smart and who doesn't like to read. Wait right here. Don't you leave, hear?"

She kind of rocked side to side to get her big body going and went back into the house.

"I really did forget," Luke whined.

I nosed my way into the pile of old clothes and got comfy. It was like walking down a city street, all the people smells in there.

When Raggedy Annie came out again, my eyes were closed. I drifted off listening to Luke sounding out words. "F-f-frozen. N-n-north." He was right, he wasn't much of a reader. But I knew he was smart. About things like that, you can't fool a smart dog.

The next two days went more or less like that. Luke wouldn't get picked, he wouldn't get the quarter, and we'd head straight over to Raggedy Annie's. I didn't always take a nap, though. I'd stick my nose into the book on Luke's lap while he sounded out the words. That's how I learned to read. It wasn't so hard. I got real caught up in that book. It was all about this great dog, Buck, and his adventures in the frozen North. It had a man in it, too. I knew Buck was going to save that man even before he did.

14

IT WAS THE LAST DAY of Adoption Week.

I crawled out from under my porch, glad to leave the noisy rats behind. Nosing my way toward the home, I thought long and hard about Luke, about why he acted the way he did, as if he didn't care if he got a home or not. I think he was afraid to show how much it meant to him. Then he could say it didn't matter when he didn't get picked. He didn't know how to change his ways, and so he probably wouldn't. Something had to happen to show the parent people what a good boy he was, and how much he needed them. I thought and thought, and finally hit upon a plan. I wasn't sure it would work, but it was worth a try. Something told me it was Luke's last chance.

All that worrying and planning had made me wander off course. I was late. Hurrying across the parking lot, I never noticed the old pickup parked there. Once again I stationed myself under the window.

The boys were in their line, hands held out so that the old gray guy could check them. Some boys had to leave the room to wash up again. Luke was one of them. I watched him slump out. He came back, wiping his hands down his pants, and went to the end of the line.

The parent people came in, two by two. They all looked like pretty good catches to me. Well fed. A little bit lonely but happy looking. And what do you know: the last ones in were the perfect parents, the same pretty lady and the man with the haystack hair.

Luke had another chance, if only he would grab it!

The gray guy gave his speech, the boys laughed when they were supposed to, and then the shaking hands stuff started. Luke went down the line dragging his feet, sticking out his hand each time as if he didn't mean to do it.

I waited until he was one boy away from the haystack guy, until he reached to shake the haystack guy's hand, then I barked.

Loud.

Everybody turned.

Mrs. Pinch's mouth fell open.

The gray guy's glasses slid down his nose.

"Jack!" cried Luke, and raced to the window.

And then I began doing my flips. Flip flip flip. Past the window and back again, flip, flip, flip.

The window flew up. Luke stuck out his head. "Jack!" Luke was laughing, laughing so hard I had to flip a couple more times.

The pretty lady and the haystack man had come to the window, too. They were smiling, watching Luke watching me.

"That's my dog!" cried Luke, grabbing the lady's hand. "His name is Jack!"

15

LUKE NEVER DID LET GO of the pretty lady's hand. Katrin her name is. He pulled her down the hall, out the door, and introduced her to me. She knelt to pet me, one-handed. Luke still had hold of the other one.

Well, Luke knows a good thing when he sees one. He just had to learn to look up.

Olaf smiled at the three of us from the window, his haystack hair shining in the sun.

It wasn't long before we were all in the pickup, Luke in the front with his new folks, me in the back where the wind ruffled my fur and I could watch the long road disappearing behind us. It took a while to get to our new place, but it was worth a sore hind end. Not since Bob and Ellen's ranch had I seen so much land in one place.

We drove up to a little house and a barn, and the first thing I smelled was sheep. Sheep! I hopped out and began rounding up the herd. All six of them. Yeah, I know, only six, but in no time they were the best-trained, most well behaved sheep in the whole world. Don't ask me how I know, I just know.

Olaf and Katrin, our folks, are just getting things going. Couple hundred acres is all. That's not much for a sheep ranch, but it's a start. Come spring we'll have our first lambs. More work for me once the silly things are up and running, but that's my job.

After a long hard workday, I sleep with Luke, down by his feet. He needs me, especially in the winter. It gets pretty cold here. Hanging from his bedpost is my old harness. I think Luke put it there to remind us how good we have it now.

Luke likes his new school, and he does his best to make Katrin and Olaf proud. Almost every day he brings something home for Katrin to stick on the refrigerator. He can read now and, boy, can he draw. Trees and sheep and trains and just about everything. He even drew a picture of me. He had to tell me it was me, but Katrin said it was a very handsome likeness and put a frame around it. It's hanging right there, over our bed.

I don't dream about the sheep anymore, which is just as well. Sheep in the daytime, sheep at night. A fella wouldn't get any rest. But one night I dreamed about the Goat Man. It was one of those dreams you know is real when you're having it. No different from real life is what I'm saying, with smells and color and sound. Like TV, only better.

In the dream, it was night. The sky was a big black bowl set down over our heads, and the silver stars hung down from it as if they were on strings.

We were camped alongside a river, the goats hunkered down, and the Goat Man was roasting some dinner over a hot fire. My mouth was watering, watching that goat's meat sizzle and smoke.

It wasn't long before he would leave us. The Goat Man didn't know he was going, of course. But maybe, just a little, he did. Because he was talking about the philosophy again, the way old folks sometimes do. Why we're on this earth, why we do what we do, all that sort of thing.

"Life's not so hard to figure out, Shep." He poked the fire. Flames shot up, the meat sizzled and spit. "Sad to say, most people don't know that. They've got to get themselves a whole pile of money, big cars, fancy houses. Run themselves ragged." He shook his head like he was mad and sad at the same time. "Truth is, a fellow doesn't need a whole lot to make him happy. A place to bed down, warm food in his belly, honest work, good company. But he's gotta have one thing more, doesn't he, boy?" I didn't know what that could be. All I needed right then was a nice, fat chunk of that meat. "A fellow's got to know he made a difference. That he used his noodle to make things a little better."

Then he gave me that special wink, like he did when he was feeling extra smart.

When I awoke from that dream, I didn't know where I was at first. I had been so many places by then that I'd wait sometimes to open my eyes. Who knew but that I'd find myself back in that terrible circus again. But there was Luke, fast asleep, his feet against my side. I cocked my ears to listen, but the Goat Man had faded away to where the memories go and wait for you to have them again.

Outside our window the moon was just a sliver, a wink in the dark sky.

Go Fish!

GOFISH

VALERIE HOBBS

What did you want to be when you grew up?
More than anything, I wanted to be a professional ice-skater.

When did you realize you wanted to be a writer?
There wasn't any one moment of realization. It just came over me sneakily, and then I realized that I was one.

What's your first childhood memory?
Sticking my finger into an open light socket. It was almost my last memory!

What's your most embarrassing childhood memory?
Running naked out of the bathroom when the lights went off into the living room full of people. Of course, the lights came right back on and there I was.

What's your favorite childhood memory?
Christmas morning, deep snow, a "real" baby carriage and doll, a miniature piano.

As a young person, who did you look up to most?
Lad, A Dog. I'm serious.

What was your worst subject in school?
Math.

What was your best subject in school?
English.

What was your first job?
Selling lady's underwear at Woolworth's.

How did you celebrate publishing your first book?
I took myself to lunch at an expensive restaurant downtown and had a glass of wine. Then I wrote notes for my next book all over the paper table cover. But I didn't write the book.

Where do you write your books?
In my "office" upstairs, which is also the TV room.

Where do you find inspiration for your writing?
Walking in Elings Park which has an ocean view and hang gliders.

Which of your characters is most like you?
They all are in some way, but Bronwyn Lewis is the most me.

When you finish a book, who reads it first?
My husband, Jack.

Are you a morning person or a night owl?
Definitely, morning.

What's your idea of the best meal ever?
Fresh-caught salmon from the Pacific Northwest, a glass of Jaffurs Syrah, and chocolate mousse for dessert.

Which do you like better: cats or dogs?
Dogs (but please don't tell Molly, my cat).

What do you value most in your friends?
Their ability to listen and to love me unconditionally.

Where do you go for peace and quiet?
My backyard.

What makes you laugh out loud?
My grandkids, Diego (six) and Rafael (two and a half). Just about everything they do cracks me up.

What's your favorite song?
"I Will Survive."

Who is your favorite fictional character?
Dorothea Brooke, *Middlemarch*.

What are you most afraid of?
Poverty.

What time of the year do you like best?
Fall (with Spring a close second).

What is your favorite TV show?
The Office.

If you were stranded on a desert island, who would you want for company?
My husband, Jack.

If you could travel in time, where would you go?
Paris, 1920.

What's the best advice you have ever received about writing?
Write from the heart.

What do you want readers to remember about your books?
We are amazing and powerful human beings, each and every one of us. Sometimes we lose our way but we can always find it again.

What would you do if you ever stopped writing?
Read. Travel. Whine a lot.

What do you like best about yourself?
My sense of humor.

What is your worst habit?
I fall into pessimism and believe that I will never write another book, or a good enough book.

What do you consider to be your greatest accomplishment?
Learning little by little to see the bright side of things.

Where in the world do you feel most at home?
Santa Barbara, California and Volcano, Hawaii.

What do you wish you could do better?
I wish I could write and illustrate a picture book.

What would your readers be most surprised to learn about you?
I once raced cars.

*K*eep reading for an excerpt from
Valerie Hobbs's **Defiance**,
available soon in paperback from Square Fish.

EXCERPT

Toby knew he was in trouble, but the cow didn't.

She just kept gazing at him with her huge brown eyes, like she was in love or something. So he went on petting her, even though he wasn't supposed to be here. His mother would have a fit if she knew. She was always having a fit about something, even out here in the country, where they were supposed to be having a vacation.

The cow was really big, and at first, when he'd stopped his bicycle to get a closer look, Toby was a little bit afraid of her. Didn't even know it was a "her" until he saw what was underneath, her huge pink udder swollen with milk. It made him think about the time at the hospital when he was just a little kid, eight or nine. How his eyes kept sliding over to the box of doctor gloves by the side of the sink. He knew very well that he wasn't supposed to touch anything, but they'd left him alone in the examining room for such a long time.

That was when Toby understood for the first time what being sick really meant. Nobody had yelled at him, not even when the glove full of water slipped from his hand and spurted out all over the room, all over the nurse who always saved him the grape Tootsie Pops. Nobody said a word. Sick kids got away with stuff.

Like this morning. When he got back to the cabin, his mother would probably threaten to ground him. Or make him return the bicycle to the shed where he'd found it. But her threats were mostly hot air. All Toby had to do was act tired or touch his side. "Are you okay, honey?" she'd say, smoothing her hand over his head. "Are you feeling all right?"

The cow's head was ten times bigger than a person's, and hanging over the fence as if she had been waiting for somebody just like Toby to come along and pet her. Somebody who didn't mind the fat blue flies that buzzed around her eyes and ears. And now she wouldn't let him go. If he tried to take his hand away, she'd bump it with her nose and make him start all over again.

It was a warm morning, growing hotter as the sun climbed the sky. Toby could feel it on his back and on the back of his neck. Sweat trickled from under his Giants cap and down the sides of his face. He let it be. The flies buzzed in circles around the cow's head, and somewhere in the distance a tractor coughed and started. The world was waking up. The cow stayed right where she was. So did Toby. Inside, there was this peaceful feeling. As if he'd never have to do another thing forever but stand here and pet this big old black-and-white cow.

Big, but skinny. Skinnier than cows were supposed to be, at least the ones he saw on TV or in books. You could see where her ribs were trying to poke through. Cows ate grass, that was one thing he knew, and this cow was standing in a whole field full. Grass and weeds and purple flowers that he thought might be clover. So why was she so skinny? Where did she live anyway? Where did she sleep? Not a barn in sight. But he'd passed a dirt driveway that had a banged-up mailbox at the end of it. Whoever didn't love this cow enough probably lived down that driveway.

He wondered what the cow was thinking about him. He was skinny, too. Tall for eleven, but she probably wouldn't know that. Maybe she was wondering about the bruises on his arms. It was hard to tell with cows.

Tomorrow he'd bring her an apple, or some Cheerios. But today, right now, he had to get home. He gave the cow one last rub between the eyes. It was still early. If his mother wasn't up yet, he could sneak the bike back into the shed.

Using the fence post for support, Toby climbed back onto the bike. Like a girl, lifting his right leg over the bar. He wished he were strong enough to leap up and land on the seat, the right way, the way the boys at school did. But at least he had a bike to ride. Pushing off with his left foot, Toby wobbled toward home.

The road stretched ahead of him into the distance. Longer than when he was coming down it, though that couldn't be. After a while, he stopped the bike, sweat running down his face, dripping from his chin. He took off his cap, pulled up his T-shirt, and wiped his whole head with it. He began to walk the bike. It was easy in the shade, but harder as the road began to climb.

It seemed to go on forever, snaking up through dappled shade. Toby watched his feet instead of the road, one sneakered foot going forward, then the other, fooling himself into thinking it wasn't so steep, or so far. All the same, he was out of breath by the time he got to the top. So beat, he thought about leaving the bike at the foot of the drive that led to their rented cabin.

But the only way to keep it for tomorrow, and all the tomorrows after that, was to hide the old bike in the shed. He bent himself into one last push, breathing hard, leaning into the worn rubber handle grips for support. And when he lifted his head, there was his mother. She was standing on the porch in her fuzzy blue bathrobe with her fists on her hips and her black curls poking out of her head like springs.

"Toby?"

Head down, Toby pushed the bike across the dry grass and laid it against the side of the cabin. It didn't have a kickstand. It didn't even have a front fender. But at least it was a bike. In the city he wasn't allowed to ride a bike. He still wasn't very good at it.

"Toby? What did I tell you, young man?"

She was eight feet tall from where he stood at the base of the steps. "You mean, about the bike?"

"You know very well what I mean. Did I *not* say you were *not* to ride the bicycle until we could get you a helmet? Did you *not* hear me say that? Toby?" He hated the way her eyebrows pinched together in the middle when she was angry.

Once, when she'd been yelling at him just like this, a bubble of laughter had started up in his belly. Because her eyebrows looked exactly like two fighting caterpillars. He'd tried his hardest to swallow down the bubble, but it tickled right up his throat and jumped out. And then he just couldn't stop. He laughed so hard he lost his breath and had to roll on the floor clutching his stomach. Which only made things worse. So now he had to not think about caterpillars, which only made him think about caterpillars.

"Yeah," he said.

Her face came down over him, pinched and white-looking. "Pardon me?"

"I mean yes. Yes, *Mother*. I heard you."

"Oh, Toby," she said, sighing her sad sigh. She frowned at him for a while without saying anything at all, her arms crossed. Then she gathered her robe around her legs and sat down on the top step, where her face was even with his. "Don't you get it, honey?" she said. "You've got to take better care of yourself. I can't be watching you all the time."

"I do take good care of myself."

"You didn't take the cell phone."

"I forgot."

"What about sunscreen? Did you at least put on sunscreen?"

Toby lied to his mother sometimes, more and more lately. It was the only way he could get her to leave him alone. But it always made him feel bad. Only weenies and bad people told lies, or so he thought before he began to tell them.

"Yup," he said, and swallowed hard.

"The number thirty?"

"Uh huh."

"All over?"

"All over."

One of her caterpillar eyebrows arched its back. "Then you must have sweated it all off because I can't smell it."

This was when he could have said, "Right! I sweated it off," or told her it was the *unscented* stuff. But the best liars knew when to keep their mouths shut. And they looked their mothers straight in the eye without flinching. Trouble was, their mothers didn't flinch either.

It seemed like forever before his mother finally stood up and said, "Come on inside. I'm making crepes."

The kitchen wasn't much of a kitchen. It didn't have a real stove for one thing. But he'd watched his mother make a ham and cheese omelet over a campfire once and knew she could cook anything, even on the little stove thing, which was just two burners that got plugged into the wall.

Butter sizzled in the frying pan. His mother tipped in the crepe batter so that it covered the bottom of the pan like a thin sheet of plastic. "Daddy called," she said. "He might not be able to make it tomorrow."

"Again?" Toby's father was supposed to drive up on Friday nights and stay the weekend. That was the plan. His father would come and they would do stuff, hike, go out on the lake. Toby would learn how to fish. But in the three weeks he and his mother had stayed in the cabin, his father had come only once. He was "knocked out," he'd said, and slept in the hammock all Saturday afternoon. Toby's mother stuck tiny tomato plants into a patch of dug-up ground. Then she got up, dusted off her knees, and went inside to practice her cello. Toby sat on the porch reading *Holes* to the somber drone of Mozart. He would have been out riding the bike, but his father had forgotten to bring him a helmet. He felt like a prisoner, like Stanley Yelnats at Camp Green Lake.

Except that there really was a lake, and it was green. Sort of furry along the sides. Algae, his father said it was. Bacteria, his mother said. And that was the end of any ideas about swimming.

Toby smeared his crepe with strawberry jam, ate a couple of bites. Then a couple more because it was easier to chew and swallow than listen to a lecture.

"Don't forget your pills," his mother said, like she always said. A zillion tablets and capsules and vitamins. Red ones, green ones, yellow ones, round ones, ones too big to swallow that had to be chopped in half, capsules with powder inside or oily liquid, big ugly brown pills that smelled like barf. One half cup. It said so right there on the plastic measuring cup his mother put them in. "We don't need you to get sick."

I'm already sick, he could have said, but didn't. It wasn't something they talked about. It was something they did. He and his mother and his father, the way other families got ready for Disneyland or Hawaii, only different. No laughing or looking forward to. There really wasn't any way to get ready for being sick. You just did it. Packed your clothes and books, your laptop. Tried not to think about the surgery and all the chemo that would come after. Three months at Children's Hospital, where other kids like him got better or worse or just disappeared, their beds made up as if they'd never been there. Toby didn't want to think about his time there now that it was over.

Only it wasn't. On the third morning after they'd settled into the cabin, Toby had felt it again. It was in the same spot on his right side, a slippery marble. He'd jumped out of bed and hurried into his clothes, covering it up.

His mom had been standing at the little kitchen sink sipping her coffee. There were purple shadows under her eyes. "Sleep all right, honey?"

"Sure."

She looked out the window. "It's going to be hot today. Did you pack your trunks?"

"My trunks?" *Was he hearing right? The lake was off-limits, wasn't it?*

"I thought you could help me for a while in the garden," she said. "Then we could . . . Oh, I don't know . . ." Her smile was lopsided, as if she was out of practice. "Run through the sprinkler to cool off! Or are you too old for that?"

"I'm eleven, Mom," he said. "Jeez!" *Run through the sprinkler? Was she nuts?* And anyway, he did have his trunks. He just couldn't wear them. Or she would see. Her eagle eyes would go straight to the marble and he would be back at Children's Hospital in no time flat. She would call an ambulance. Or get a helicopter. Only he wasn't going to do all that again. He wasn't going to puke up his guts over and over while his mother held his head. He wasn't going to miss school and lose what few friends he had left. He wasn't going to make new friends with kids who disappeared. It would be the biggest lie he'd ever told, and he would tell it over and over again whenever she asked him how he was, no matter how bad it made him feel.

"Fine," he'd tell her. "I'm fine."